S0-CCE-282

FIC
DIL

DATE DUE

OCT 11			

THE SEALS

Other books by the same author

THE SEALS

By Eilís Dillon

Illustrated by Richard Kennedy

FUNK & WAGNALLS   New York

2041

1

contents

THE SEALS

chapter 1 ~~~~~~~~~~~~~~~~~~~~~~~~~~~~

A Storm

All day long, the sky had been darkening over the island. It had been a clear morning, with the blue curves of the Clare mountains plainly visible.

"They're too plain," old Morgan the weaver said. "When you can see the walls of Clare like that, there's a storm coming. And the sea gulls have moved in. They're all around the house this minute, driving me out of my mind with their squalling."

It was true that in the afternoon the island had suddenly become covered with little groups of huddled white and gray and black-backed gulls, shrieking dismally to each other though the sun still shone.

"Bad luck to them and their howling," said Jim Conneeley, who was Pat's father and Morgan's son. "They always have the bad story."

"We should be thankful to them," said old Morgan excitedly. "Where would we be without them? They're there to give warning. The sea gulls are never wrong. Many a life they've saved, you can take it from me——"

"All right, Father. Sure I was only joking," said Jim. "It's only that I wish they had a more civil way of announcing the storm. To listen to them, you'd think we'd all be better to shut ourselves in our houses and barricade the doors and build up the fires and wait for the big wind to blow the roof off. You'd never think we'd have time to take in the lobster pots and put the boats safe before the storm strikes."

While he was talking, he was taking the oars of the currach from their place by the back door and picking up a coil of new rope from the chest beside the fire. He passed one pair of oars to Pat to carry. Before they were on the doorstep, the old man said:

"Mind that wind! It's coming up very fast though you wouldn't think it."

"We'll mind everything," said Jim.

Out on the road he said:

"We'll call in for Mike Hernon. He might have a few pots out."

Pat was very pleased with this. He had been hoping his father would suggest it. Mike was his great friend, though he was two years older than Pat. Perhaps because he had had to do a man's work for several years, he seemed to have the ways and the experience of a man. His father had been lost at sea when Mike was ten years old, and he had quietly and naturally taken over all the work on the land and with the lobster fishing, as if there were nothing unusual in it. Pat admired him very much, and had once or twice wondered if he himself would have been so efficient if the need arose.

Without the help of his neighbors, of course, Mike would have been quite lost. They helped him with the spring sowing and with the potato harvest. They advised him when it was time to sell his young cattle. They came around with straw and long ladders when the thatching was due in September. And they always saw to it that someone was ready to help lay his lobster pots at the same time as their own.

Mike was at his door when they reached it, looking down the hill toward the sea.

" 'Twill be a storm, all right," Jim said to him. "We're going after the pots. Let you come with us and we'll bring them all in together."

Mike's mother came trotting around the corner of the house in her bare feet. She had been out in the wet grass, bringing their food to the pigs. She was a young woman still, but she had a perpetually sad look about her which made her seem older.

"Good man, Jim," she said, "and the blessings of God on you. May ye all come safe."

As they went on down the hill, her prayers and benedictions followed them. Secretly Pat was glad that his own mother did not do this. He knew that she prayed all the time while he and his father were at sea, but he knew too that she did it quietly, so that a stranger would never have guessed it.

Though the wind was freshening every moment, it was not cold. Summer storms were never as wicked as the winter ones, which seemed to tear and bite like maddened sharks. But the summer storms were just as dangerous, in their way. That warm wind was quite strong enough to lift a boat out of the sea and dash it to pieces on the rocks. Away out on the horizon now, they could see white-pointed waves dancing in the sun. Black clouds were piling up above the sea to the west.

"Time enough," Jim said comfortably. "We'll have the pots ashore before that reaches us."

Down on the beach, several men were busy launching their currachs. They never hurried at anything, except when they were doing this. At every other kind of work, the arrival of a friend was enough excuse for the pipes to be taken out and a long, restful conversation to begin. Now they barely called out a greeting:

"Hóra, Jim! After the pots, are you?"

Then they got on with their business, giving it all their attention. The currach had to be carried into the water until the men were splashing up to their knees. Then they quickly dropped it and skipped aboard, and with one or two strokes of the oars took it out beyond the breakers.

Pat and Mike took one side of the currach, while Jim took the other. The shelving sand seemed to slip dizzily away under their feet and the currach seemed to weigh a ton. Then suddenly it was afloat and they were skimming up and over the waves, down into the hollows between, and out to the smoother waters beyond.

The floats of the lobster pots were prancing a quarter of a mile off shore, and they sent the currach flying toward them.

"We're in luck that the tide is in," Jim said. "The reef is well covered. If we're blown, we'll go in on the sand."

The sea above the reef always seemed to be the first to turn black when a storm was coming. The pots had to be laid near it because the lobsters liked it there. Jim said:

"We'll take in Mike's pots first. They're the farthest out."

The boys knew that there was another reason—that though the reef was covered, if the storm came down fast it

could not be approached at all. Jim wanted to make sure that if one string of pots was lost, it would not be Mike's.

Lifting the pots into the currach was a slow business. Each one was weighted with stones to make it sink. While the boys handled the oars, Jim leaned over the stern of the currach and hauled on the line. One by one, he raised the pots to the surface and lifted them aboard. It was man's work, because they weighed even more heavily when they were no longer supported by the water. Mike had six pots, and when they were all aboard the currach, it was top-heavy and far too low in the water.

Jim watched anxiously while the boys rowed for the shore, much more slowly now, with creaking oarlocks, and splashes of sea continually coming over the gunwale. He kept his hands on the pots, in which several lobsters crouched.

"You have a nice little catch, Mike," he said. "And you'll get a good price for them if you can keep them alive until the boats come."

Mike gave a snort. "When will that be, I wonder? They'll be grandfather lobsters by the time I get to selling them, if the war doesn't stop soon."

"You know the boats keep coming anyway, whenever they can. And sure, the war must stop some time," Jim said quietly. "We ought to be thankful we don't see much of it out here on the islands."

The year was 1920 and throughout the country a terrible struggle was raging. During seven hundred years, Ireland had fought for independence from English rule. Now success was only two years away, but the tired and dispirited people did not know it. Naturally they thought that this was going to be just another link in the chain of disasters that had afflicted their country for so long: the lost battles of Kinsale and Aughrim, the savage campaigns of Cromwell and Marlborough, the crushed uprisings of 1798 and 1916, with dozens of minor incidents each of which should have driven the people further into depressed slavery.

But for some reason, they had never been enslaved. There was always a leader, and there were always songs of hope to light up their spirits again and to start the usual pattern of plot and rising and death and defeat.

This time, the defeat did not seem to be coming so quickly. The terrible army of desperadoes, known as the Black and Tans, was doing its best to terrorize the people, burning houses and whole villages, torturing and killing and raiding. But this time the usual effect was not achieved. Instead of giving up in despair, the people stiffened their resistance in face of these horrors. They knew it had all happened before, because in Ireland history is so real as to seem unconnected with time. A man can lament for the Flight of the Earls as if it were only last week they went off to Rome and left the country leaderless, though this happened in 1607. A man could say of the Black and Tans:

"They're a lot worse than Cromwell's army. They were only walking through the country. You'd have time to run from them when you'd hear them coming. But these blackguards with their lorries are inside in the yard before you know it."

Perhaps it was the knowledge of thousands of long-dead heroes that supported the Irish now. They fought back, mostly with carefully planned ambushes in hilly country, striking suddenly at the convoys of lorries and then retreating back into the hills again as best they could. How long this would serve, no one could tell.

" 'Tis true, we don't see much of it here," Mike said, and Pat said softly:

"I wish we saw more of it. I wish we weren't so far out at sea and we could do something small, even, just to be in it."

"It's not our job," Jim said. "You know I asked Roddy if we should go over to Galway and he said we'd be no use, with the kind of fighting that's going on. He said the Tans would spot an islandman a half-mile away. They'd be after us like wasps. And they'd be out to the island then, killing all around them."

"I know, I know," said Pat.

Roddy was Pat's uncle, Jim's brother. Everyone knew that he was the bravest fighter and the most wanted man in all Connemara. His greatest value was that he was unknown there, being an islandman. Descriptions of him had been circulated—one hung in the island post office at that moment, to the great amusement of everyone—but not even his name was known to the authorities. All they knew was that when a certain stranger had been about, the ambushes were more expertly planned.

Many times Pat had thought of slipping off and joining this wonderful uncle, but he was old enough to know that he might not get a great welcome. Apart from his feelings about this, he knew that he might actually harm the men who were fighting for their very existence. Wars of this kind had no rooms for boys, though there had been a place for them earlier.

Jim said:

"When the good times come again, they say that we'll have bigger boats, with engines, for the lobster pots."

There was no more talk then. The wind had strengthened, though not very much. It was useful to them now, making their progress to the shore faster. Soon they were at the beach, floundering in the waves, soaked up to their armpits, carefully dragging the loaded currach as far out of the water as they could without scraping her heavily on the shingly sand. They laid the lobster pots out of reach of the sea, strewing the cork floats on top of them in their hurry. Then they set out for their second load.

This time they worked faster. With easy, loosened muscles they sent the currach flying and within a few minutes they were hauling in the first of Jim's pots. The sky was blackening over now, and there was a little whistle in the wind. Off toward the Connemara shore they could see the full black sails of a hooker.

"If that fellow has any sense he's on his way home," Jim said. "This is no day for a sail."

His lobster pots were well-filled too. As he lifted them aboard, he said:

"I hope the boat will come soon, indeed. I'm always afraid that if it delays long enough, some day Maggie will say we might as well eat the lobsters ourselves. I'm hoping to go to God without ever tasting one. They're a queer class of food—they're neither fish nor flesh."

Pat was curious about lobsters, however, and often wished they could have eaten one if only to try it. His mother knew very well how to cook them, from her years in Boston when she was a young girl. Like most of the island girls, she had gone off to America for a few years, before she married, to earn her dowry and to see the world. She knew that lobsters are good food but what her husband wanted was law to her and he had often said that he would as soon put Shep the dog into the pot as a lobster. So Pat knew he would have to wait a long time to satisfy his curiosity.

The waves had grown while they were taking the pots aboard. They followed them hungrily, showing their teeth, all the way back to the strand. The sea had suddenly turned

lead-colored and was full of little whirling columns of bub-
bles and sand stirred up from the bottom. The boys knew
better than to look down at it. They kept their eyes on their
toes and pulled their strongest. Jim's anxious face told them
without words that they should save their breath for the
oars.

They could see that they were the last at sea. The other
currachs that had gone out after pots had only had one load
each. For some reason, it was rather frightening to be alone
on that ugly sea, though the sight of the other boats in danger would not have helped to reduce their own. This
thought sent a shiver down Pat's spine, or perhaps it was
caused by his wet clothes, chilled by the wind.

At the beach, of course, several of the men were ready to
haul them ashore.

"Good work, Jim," they said, as satisfied as if the lobsters
were their own. "Not a pot lost. Every one safe."

"And I didn't need my new rope," Jim said. "The lines
held fine. 'Twill do for another day."

Rope was precious stuff, like everything that had to be
bought and paid for on the mainland.

Jim's wife, Maggie, was waiting with the donkey-cart at
the top of the beach.

"When I came in from the cows, Morgan told me where
you were gone," she said. "God in heaven, there's a
storm!"

She turned her back on it as she always did. Maggie never
went to sea if she could avoid it. Sometimes when she was
promised a week of fine weather by every expert on the island, she would venture in to Galway on the steamer to do
some shopping. All the way there and back, she would sit
motionless in a place from which the sea was invisible,
wrapped tightly in her shawl and praying without ceasing

for the safety of the whole concern. It was not that she had no courage, just that she did not believe in taking unnecessary risks.

When the cart was loaded high with all the pots, she whacked the donkey to encourage him to move. He turned his head and glared, feeling the weight of the double load. When he saw Maggie, he moved off, knowing it was useless to resist.

The boys helped Jim to carry the currach well above the beach. They laid it upside down under the shelter of a low wall. Then they brought heavy stones and placed them carefully against the gunwales so that it could not blow away. Jim turned to look out to sea.

"There's three or four days in that storm at the very

least," he said. "It will probably ease off a bit tomorrow and then blow up again."

"How do you know that sort of thing?" Pat asked.

"Experience. And all the Conneeleys know the sea." He laughed suddenly. "Do you know what they say about us? They say that all the Conneeleys are really seals that came ashore and set up house, and after a while they grew arms and legs and began to look like real people. Did you ever hear that?"

"I heard it," said Mike.

"Of course you did," said Jim. "But Pat didn't, you see. Am I right, Pat?"

"I never heard it," said Pat.

"You see," Jim said, "people wouldn't say it to a Conneeley's face though they'd think of it, all right. I don't see any harm in it, myself. We're people now, for sure, and not seals, whatever our ancestors were. And it could be mighty useful to have some seal's blood in you. They say the Conneeleys can't be drowned, because of it. Sure enough, you never heard of a Conneeley being drowned."

Pat could see that his father was laughing at the whole story and yet he was not quite sure whether there might not be some truth in it. There were only four families of Conneeleys on the island and every member of them was a good swimmer. Most of the islanders could not swim at all and did not even want to try. It was true that no Conneeley had ever been lost at sea, that Pat had ever heard of. And none of them were afraid of the sea, not even the women. Pat's mother was a Folan from Eochaill, so she didn't count.

All the way up to the houses he thought about it. He would have liked to ask Mike whether he believed the old story, but Mike looked too old and sensible to be asked such foolish questions.

chapter 2

A Stranger

At Mike's house they found the donkey-cart waiting. Maggie had gone inside to have a chat with Mrs. Hernon. The donkey shivered in the wind, which was blowing his fur up in little tufts. It was blowing the sand along the road too, lifting it and whirling it here and there. On a good day there would still have been an hour of daylight but now it seemed that night was about to fall.

"I hate a storm in August," Jim said as they lifted Mike's lobster pots off the cart. "It brings the winter down on us before its time."

This was true, but now suddenly Pat remembered the lighted kitchen on winter's nights, with the turf fire glowing and the neighbors gathered in for long, slow, leisurely talks.

"You'll come over to our place this evening," he said to Mike. "The fire will be stoked up, I'm sure."

At that moment Maggie appeared at the door with Mrs. Hernon saying:

"Let ye all come over to our place this evening for a while. We'll have a fine fire and good talk."

Mrs. Hernon's glum face brightened at this and she said:

"We'll come, indeed, and God bless you."

Mike said quietly to Pat:

"We'll be there for sure. All the sport will be inside as long as the storm lasts."

After supper, Maggie brushed the hearth clean and arranged old Morgan's high-backed chair to one side of it. His was the corner away from the doors, so that he was never in a draft. There were four doors to the kitchen. There was the front door with a half-door as well, which could be closed to keep the chickens out and let the air in. There was the back door, which was always closed except when the wind was at the front of the house. In winter it was covered with a heavy mat of woven straw, to keep out the drafts. As well as these there were the two bedroom doors, one at either side of the kitchen.

Above Morgan's chair the oil lamp hung on the wall, with its tin reflector glowing brightly. On a bracket nearby, a little red-globed lamp burned day and night in front of the holy picture. High on the mantel above the fire, in shining frames and with shining glass, were several photographs of aunts and uncles in America. Maggie said of them that one and all looked as if they had swallowed the poker, they seemed so stiff and startled. But she said it didn't matter because she would always remember them as they were in Ireland, young and cheerful and lively. Two white china dogs with round staring eyes sat at either end of the mantel, and there were two tall blue vases as well, with gold and roses on them.

Altogether it was a beautiful kitchen, and Pat was always proud of it when visitors came in. Mike and his mother came together, and while Maggie was fussing with a chair for Mrs. Hernon, old John Faherty appeared in the doorway.

"God save all here," he said. "Where's Morgan?"

Every evening that he came—and that was most evenings—he said the same thing. He and Morgan had been at school together, so they said. Pat could hardly imagine them at school, they were both so tall and straight and dignified. What teacher would dare to put them in the corner for chatting during a lesson on South America, or for fighting in the yard at lunch time? He tried to imagine them small and dirty and wicked, like all the boys on the island, but he just could not.

"Morgan is at the loom," Maggie said. "Run out, Pat, and call him in."

Pat loved going to the weaving shed. The loom was as dignified and precise as Morgan. It moved neatly and accurately up and down as he worked the pedals from a tall stool. It made a soft whirring noise and then a clack as the shuttles fell into place. Morgan let it go silent as soon as he saw Pat. The noise of the wind seemed to grow louder.

"John Faherty is here," Pat said. "The fire is made up. My mother said you've worked enough."

Old Morgan got down stiffly from the stool. He stretched himself tall and wide, so that his shadow in the lamplight scuttled across the ceiling like a huge spider. He turned the lamp down until it went out with a quiet flicker. Then they went outside, locking the door carefully behind them. The door of the weaving shed must have been the only locked door on the whole island. Morgan was always rather apologetic about it.

"It's not that I think anyone would touch it," he said to Pat once. "It's just that a loom should never be behind an open door. I learned that when I was an apprentice in Donegal. They're very precious about their cloth up there—much more than we are—always afraid someone will work a wrong thread into a piece and ruin it all. Now I have a kind of habit of locking the door and I suppose I'll be that way until I die."

From the doorstep of the shed, they could look all the way down the hill to the sea. Darkness had fallen but somewhere among the galloping clouds there was a moon. It picked out spots of light and dark on the ocean, making it huge and terrible. Just as they turned toward the house, Pat thought he saw a light on a masthead out there. He flew into the kitchen in fright. Nothing but a ghost ship could survive in that sea. From everything he had ever heard of them, Pat knew that he wanted no truck with ghosts.

In the kitchen his mother said:

"What's on you? You look as if you saw a ghost."

"It's the wind. It howls like a banshee," Pat said weakly.

He sat on top of the great blanket chest with Mike. Slowly and deliberately, Morgan and John took their places at either side of the fire. Maggie settled on the hob with the sock she was knitting, and Jim had his usual chair near the turf-stack, so that he could make up the fire from time to time as it needed it. Suddenly Jim said:

"You'd think 'twas winter. What's the world coming to when we have a storm like this in the height of summer?

Look at us, sitting around the fire like Christmas night!"

"Times haven't changed much," said Morgan. "I remember many a summer as bad as this and worse."

"So do I," said old John Faherty. " 'Twas in the month of July that we got the cargo of mahogany when I was eleven years old. That was a great storm. We never saw the ship the mahogany came on. Maybe it went down fifty miles out to sea. But we got bales and bales of timber, rolling in on every tide, until we thought we'd be building in shingles like they do in America if it went on long enough. Every house on the island got new rafters out of it and most got a new dresser."

Old John had spent fifteen years in America when he was young. He had worked on whaling ships that went out from Maine, which he said was not very different from Connemara. This fact had made it easier for him to come home when the time came.

"And it was in August that the big storm broke up the lighthouse in Buntarna, forty-one years ago to the minute. The waves were as big as any I ever saw in winter," Morgan said. "They went up over the top of it and broke it in two, like you'd break a pencil."

"What happened to the lightkeepers?" Mike asked.

"They got ashore before the worst of it. They rigged up a temporary light on the cliff to warn any ships that might come, but sure no ship in her senses would come that close unless she was helpless. And if she was helpless, the light wouldn't be much good to her."

Pat thought of the light he had seen. In the warm, bright kitchen he had the courage to ask:

"Did you ever hear of a ghost ship?"

"Ghost ship?" his father asked sharply. "Where did you hear that nonsense?"

"At Lynskeys', on Sunday evening. They were all talking about it."

"The Lynskeys haven't an ounce of sense among the lot of them. What did they say?"

"That the ghost ship comes in a storm. That it can sail along in the wildest sea. That whoever sees it will be drowned at sea before the year is out."

"God save us all! That's unchristian talk."

"It's wicked talk, before young boys too."

"I hope you didn't believe it."

By this time Pat wished he had said nothing. He knew that the Lynskeys were thought to be foolish people. Owen Lynskey and his wife Kate owned a nice little piece of land, as good as any on the island. But they never did anything with it. The only crop they planted was potatoes—and never enough of them. By May of every year, their son Jerry was appearing at each door in the island in turn, with a basket and an apologetic smile, asking for a few spuds for their dinner.

Sometimes a woman would get sorry for Kate and bring her a clutch of eggs and a clocking hen, with a fierce injunction against eating either. But when the chickens hatched out, they went into the pot one by one, and the hen after them, so that within a few months the family was back where it started. For milk they depended entirely on their neighbors. Once they had owned a cow but even the heifer calves had been sold, so that when the cow died in old age there had been no young one ready to succeed her.

Owen Lynskey spent all day, except when it rained, leaning on the wall in front of his house and chatting with anyone who passed by. The first glimpse of his house always included the tassel of his cap, just as the first view of Buntarna always included the lighthouse. At night he sat by his own fire telling stories about the giants and heroes of ancient Ireland, and about the fairies and banshees and pookas of the present day. He liked an audience but if no one else came he told it all quite happily to his wife and son. They watched his face and listened as eagerly as if it were all news to them, though surely they could have recited any of those stories backwards by this time.

"Owen is a wonder at the stories," Kate used to say. "There's some are all for planting and sowing, and some for raising cattle and sheep, and some for fishing lobster and herring to get rich and fat, but Owen only cares for the stories. And sure we get on fine as we are, with the help of God and our neighbors."

The neighbors could say nothing to this, though from time to time they tried to teach young Jerry the virtue of work. It was not easy to do it without seeming to criticize his father. That they would never have done.

Morgan said:

"Owen Lynskey has a great memory for stories, indeed. It's a long time since I heard that one about the ghost ship. My father had it, and I think he half-believed it. Of course it's nothing but nonsense."

"What else did your father have?" old John asked. "Did he have the piece about the knocks on the door, to call out the man that was to be drowned?"

Jim shifted in his chair and looked uneasily at the boys. Of course he could not tell his own father and his father's old friend to have sense, but one could see he wished they would not talk like this. He never liked talk of superstitions. He said there were enough dangers in the real world all around, without inventing new ones, and that he had never in his life known them to come true.

"I heard my father talk of knocks on the door, all right,"

said Morgan. "Three knocks there would be, always on a stormy night. Slow knocks. You'd go to the door and there would be no one there." He stretched his legs and said comfortably: "I do often think that people were more simple in the long-ago times. It was a queer thing because they were always travelers in the islands. My father sailed the China Sea, and went ashore whenever he got the chance, to see the wonders of all those foreign places."

"Sailors have the worst stories," Jim said. "They seem to be afraid of their own shadows."

Then it came, quite distinctly above the noise of the wind that was roaring in the chimney. Three loud knocks, with a little break between. Pat felt as if he would never be able to move again. The old men sat up straight and looked at each other without expression. Maggie dropped her knitting and blessed herself. Mrs. Hernon gave a little squeak of terror. After one second's hesitation, Jim sprang across the kitchen and opened the door. Mike was only a moment behind him.

As he remembered it afterwards, Pat's worst moment was when the door was thrown open and there was no one standing there. The wind whirled in and sent up a cloud of turf ashes. The red curtains on the window blew out into the room. The flame of the lamp climbed all the way up the globe, staining it with soot.

Then Jim was out on the doorstep with Mike. From inside the kitchen they could be seen stooping together and lifting something. With slow, careful steps they carried their load into the house and laid it down.

Mike shut the door. Maggie said:

"God help us! It's a man. Is he drowned?"

"How could he be drowned? Didn't he knock at the door?"

"He's a stranger. That's the Connemara tweed," said the
weaver. He got up and said sharply:

"Put him in my chair. A drop of something, Maggie. He
didn't come here for his health. Come on, man! You'll be
all right when you have something to warm you."

They lifted him like a sack and sat him in Morgan's tall-
backed chair. Then Jim straightened him up so that his face
was visible for the first time.

With a great sense of relief, Pat saw that the man's eyes

were open and he was looking at the little half-circle of people who were watching him with curiosity. He was a powerfully built man with reddish gold hair and thick eyebrows. Just now his face was as white as the kitchen wall. He was dressed in the gray and white trousers, of the tweed called glasheen caorach, that all the Connemara people used to wear at that time. He had a navy blue fisherman's jersey and over it a white báanín jacket. All of these marked him as a Connemara man, and yet there was some special look of refinement and authority about him which suggested a more comfortable heredity.

Maggie pushed a mug of hot poteen and water into his hand.

"There's plenty of sugar in it," she said. "Let you drink that up and you'll be twice the man. Give him time, now," she said to the others. "Don't hurry him. Jim, make up the fire there. Sit over on the hob, Morgan. You boys get back where you were and keep as quiet as mice."

Mrs. Hernon sat back in her chair, never taking her eyes off the stranger. Maggie went across to the window and straightened the curtains that had been blown by the wind. She took great care to close them, so that even if anyone were out on such a night they would not be able to see into the kitchen. Then she pulled out a creepie stool for herself and sat down with her hands expectantly on her knees. She would never have urged the stranger in words to hurry with his story but her attitude made it quite clear to him that the moment for it had come.

He had taken two mouthfuls of his drink, lifting the mug slowly as if it were heavy. Now he drew a long, shuddering breath and said:

"I'm in the right house. You are Morgan Conneeley, the weaver?"

"That's right," Morgan said. "You've seen Roddy."

The man nodded.

"He's not wounded?" Morgan asked sharply.

"No, no. He's as well as myself—or as well as I was when I set out."

He gave a little laugh, good to hear. His voice was strong and clear, like a singer's, and he had the drawl of Connemara, stretching every vowel to twice its length.

"Before we go any further, how do you know me?" Morgan asked.

"You haven't changed much in fifteen years. I was here with my father when I was a young lad, though never since then. That's why I was sent—because I knew the island."

"Your name?"

"James Fitzmaurice."

"From Tully Cross?"

"From the Joyces's country. It's near three hundred years since the Joyces took us in, when we were driven west of the Shannon by that limb of Satan, Cromwell. We had fat land in Tipperary and North Cork, I hear, though I wasn't there at the time."

"Fitzmaurice? Would your father be Séamus Rua?"

"That's his name. I was Séamus myself until I went to school and they put a foreign name on me."

"Is your father well?"

"He is, faith. Well and strong."

"And when did you come here? Have you been in hiding, in some cave on the high shore, maybe, or in someone's sheep hut on the hill? Maybe that's why you're worn out——" Already Maggie was making up her own story, instead of waiting to hear the stranger's.

"I was not in hiding," he said. "I came straight up here from the boat."

"God preserve us! You came in a boat, on a night like this!"

Morgan said quietly:

"Finish up your drink, young fellow, and tell us your story. Everyone else can be silent until we've heard it."

chapter 3 〜〜〜〜〜〜〜〜〜〜〜〜〜〜〜〜〜〜

An Old Story

"Begin at the beginning," said Morgan. "Who sent you here? And why did you have to come?"

"Roddy sent me. As you must know, he has been living like a fox on the mountainside. There's many a one would be glad to lay hands on him. But he has as many dens as a fox, where he can lie safe. His friends know where to find him. There's good money offered to anyone that will betray him, but so far he has escaped."

"So far? Has he been captured?"

"If he had been, could I tell you he's in good health? The Tans are after him. That's what brought me here. We had a spy. We know who he is, but he got away before we found him out. He took a photograph of Roddy. We know that. Never mind how we know it. He was one of those quiet, knowledgeable people, traveled and all. Queer thing about them is that they're demon fighters, the ones we have in the movement. We don't know what got into this fellow— maybe he wanted the money, God help him. We know he got money for the photograph. It's not a very good one but it might be dangerous."

"You know a lot about that photograph."

"It's my business to know. They'll print it, and they'll have it stuck up on every wall by the end of the week."

"What do you want us to do?"

"Someone should go over to Lettermore and fetch Roddy out here, in my boat."

"Why did he not come with you?"

"He wasn't ready. He's on a job in Galway this minute, a big ambush at Oranmore. Then he's to go out to Connemara and wait for the boat in Lettermore. They were on my tail already. I couldn't wait for him, or neither of us would ever get here."

"Thanks be to God, he'll be resting for a few months then," said Morgan.

James gave a short laugh, like a fox's bark.

"Resting? He will not, then. The only reason he's coming to the island is that he wants to be sure to be free for the next ambush. There's them that go on the run for fear of being caught, but he's not like that. When the time is ripe, we'll go back together. By that time my arm will be mended."

"Your arm? What's wrong with your arm?"

"A piece of His Majesty's lead got caught in it at the last ambush but we got it out. We have to do a lot of our own repairs. It's a bad spot to have it, though. There's not much you can do with one arm only, and that the left one."

"Young fellow," said Morgan, "will you tell me something: did you sail out from Connemara in a hooker, with one arm only?"

"I did," said James. "And maybe that's why I was a bit under the weather, like, when I arrived. Sometimes I used to have to hold a sheet with that hand, and when I did, it was like seven devils were at me with pincers. I could never have moored the boat only that there was a young lad down by the quay and he helped me. He showed me the way up the road too, though I had nearly remembered it. And indeed I'm sorry, ma'am, for the way I knocked at your door. I frightened the heart in every one of you."

"Don't mind that, a-mac, as long as you're safe," said Maggie.

"Safe, indeed," said James.

Suddenly he stopped. He looked sharply at each person in the room. Then he asked in a soft voice:

"Is everyone here on our side?"

"Yes," said Morgan. "Everyone on the island is on our side."

"What about the boys?"

"They were Fenians before they were born."

"Why did Mrs. Conneeley close the curtains so carefully if everyone on the island is the right kind?"

Morgan looked uncomfortable.

"We have one family—there's no harm in them but there's no good in them either—we're never sure——"

"What is their name?"

"I wouldn't like to name them. We could be wrong about them."

"I'll allow for all that. We can't trust entirely to love in this war. You'd better tell me."

"It's the Lynskeys," Morgan said reluctantly. "All belonging to them were airy. Owen Lynskey's grandfather was an old man when I was a boy, and he never did a stroke of work in his life."

"How did he live, then?"

"Poorly enough. Then suddenly he wasn't short of money any more. People used to wonder where he got it. They knew he had sons in America but he never got a letter from them. Only once in three months he'd go to Galway and he'd come back jingling with gold."

"Gold!"

"Gold it was in those days. He'd stand a drink or two and he'd have one himself, but he never let on where he got it. The people found out, of course, after a while. Someone followed him up to the Police Barracks in Galway. 'Twas the only place he went. He sneaked in and out like a rat after a clutch of eggs. They knew then that it wasn't the leprechauns were keeping him in gold. That was long before my time, of course."

Though he and Mike had been told to be quiet, Pat could not stop himself from asking:

"What was it? Who was giving him the money?"

" 'Twas secret service money," Morgan explained. "It's always there for paying spies with. The Land War was on all over Ireland and I suppose old Lynskey persuaded the Royal Irish Constabulary that he'd give some information in return for the money. But sure, we never had much trouble with landlords here. In Aran they did, but never here. The reason he got paid at all was that his cousin was the Chief Constable."

"So the bad drop is in the Lynskeys," James Fitzmaurice said. "But you don't think the present generation is at the same game?"

"They certainly haven't got any gold," Jim said with a laugh, "unless they have some left over from the big haul."

"What was that?"

"Just once, and once only, old Lynskey had some information to give," Morgan said. "We had a lot of Aran lads
sheltering here, after a fight with the R.I.C. A widow
woman over there was being evicted and they came to
knock the house down. She hadn't a penny piece to pay the
rent with, of course. Where would she get it? And she had a
few children, but not one old enough to lift a hand for her.
So the lads said they'd make a fight of it anyway, and they
did. Afterwards they were marked, so they came over here
for the good of their health.

"There were five of them. I remember them well, though
I was only six years old at the time. And I remember the day
that a boat came out from Galway, and the police walked
straight to the houses where the lads were staying and took
them away in chains. They came with an escort of soldiers.
There wasn't a thing we could do. But I'll never forget their
faces, the longest day I live.

"My father told me there was a conference on the island
after the lads were taken away. The people knew well that
it was old Lynskey had brought the soldiers. He had sailed
over by himself to Galway with his story. After that, the
islandmen told him he could go there no more. No man
would ever drink with him again. No one went near his
house unless there was someone sick or dying. No one
would even kneel near him in the chapel on Sundays. It
sounds bad, but it could have been worse. They never gave
his name as the spy, either, as long as he lived. If they had,
someone would have come over from Aran and put an end
to him. He lived to be ninety-two and he got very religious
in the latter end."

"What was the big haul you spoke of?"

"He must have got plenty on the last trip to Galway,"

old Morgan said. "For years after, his wife used to come to the shop with a gold sovereign for the groceries." He chuckled. "I believe Luke the Shop always dipped it in Holy Water before he put it in the till."

"And what are the Lynskeys like now?"

"They're soft kind of people," Jim said. "I don't believe they'd hurt a fly. But everyone knows the old story about them so they never put their trust in any of them."

Pat had heard before that there had been a spy in the Lynskey family once, but he had never heard the whole story until now. Suddenly and without meaning to, he felt pity for Jerry Lynskey. It seemed ridiculous that he should be blamed for the sin of his great-grandfather. No one would have thought of judging a dog like that. He could be accounted a good, hard-working dog even if his great-grandfather had been a sheep-killer, so why should it not be the same for a boy?

James Fitzmaurice was saying:

"I don't think we're in much danger from those people. Still it's no harm to be extra careful. Now I need someone to sail my boat to Lettermore tomorrow. It will take two men, indeed, with a sea like this."

There was a pause and then Morgan said delicately:

"You came alone, you said?"

"I did, and hard work it was. I didn't have time to wonder if I'd get here alive. When the devil is after you, you don't think of those things."

Jim sat forward on the edge of his chair.

"You left your boat at the slip."

"Yes, and a neat little harbor it is. I left her tied up to the two bollards."

At this it seemed to Pat that the storm had suddenly become fiercer. It was the thought of the little hooker that made the wind grow louder and the roar of the waves nearer. His father was saying:

"When is Roddy expecting the boat?"

"Tomorrow evening. We have friends right by the quay at Lettermore. He'll be safe there until you come."

"For how long will he be safe?"

"He's never safe for long anywhere. Even in Lettermore someone might recognize him and turn him in for the reward. If the Tans catch him——"

"I know, I know. Listen to the wind."

Everyone listened. It was easy to see how the old stories came to be made, of demons and fairies riding on the wind, laughing and singing and shouting to each other. Every now and then it seemed to catch the house between enormous hands and shake it.

" 'Tis a powerful wind," said James Fitzmaurice after a moment.

"What can we do?" Jim said. "Roddy is my own brother. I'd swim to Lettermore for him, if I could. I'd set out in the boat for him tomorrow, but I know as sure as I'm sitting here that I wouldn't get beyond the reef, with the sea that's running. And where would I get a man to go with me, even if I were foolhardy enough to try?"

"I'd go with you," said Pat.

"You would," said Morgan delightedly. "Good man, yourself!"

"Good man, indeed," said Jim, "but we'd never get there alive. I know the sea around here as well as I know my own potato fields. It would be madness to go."

"Our whole war is madness," said James. "Our soldiers are farmers and fishermen and city clerks and students. Our arms are fifty years old. Our ammunition is mostly songs and ballads about the heroes of other days."

"But when you plan an ambush, you don't plan certain death for all your men."

"That's true, indeed. We'd gain nothing at all if we were to go tomorrow. You'd lose your life, and I'd lose the boat that may be my only way out of the island later on."

But these reasonable words were spoken in a low, depressed tone that was heartbreaking to hear. Pat noticed, however, that his mother and Mrs. Hernon glanced at each other out of the corners of their eyes, unable to cover up their satisfaction that the plan of sailing to Lettermore was to be abandoned for the moment.

Maggie lifted the sputtering kettle off the crane over the fire and set it in the ashes. Then she got down her best luster teapot, that was only used for weddings and funerals, and her best cups with the roses, and her milk jug with "A Present from Galway" written on it in gold. More than this she could not have done for anyone. She cut slices of soda-bread too, so that everyone would go to bed feeling comfortable inside.

After the tea, old John Faherty stood up and said:

"Thanks to be God we're still breeding men like yourself in Ireland, James. I'll be down the road with you, Mrs. Hernon. Come along, Mike, or we'll all be lying in bed in the morning."

Mike and Pat broke off the private talk they had been having together, sitting on top of the chest. Pat said softly:

"Don't lie in bed in the morning, whatever you do."

"I will not," said Mike.

When the door was opened to let the visitors out, the wind went thundering past like a hundred galloping horses.

Maggie said, "You can sleep in the kitchen, James, in the settle bed. You can stoke up the fire during the night, if you like. Now show me your arm."

With his good hand, James opened up the sleeve of his jersey, which had been slit and then laced with a shoelace to cover the thick bandage. Carefully Maggie dressed it for him, so expertly that he said in admiration:

"You should be with the army."

Maggie said briskly:

"Let you rest yourself there now and don't mind your army."

All night long, the wind roared around the island, as if it were trying the doors and windows in the hope of getting in. Pat heard it in the room behind the fire where he slept with his grandfather, and he shivered when he thought of the little hooker moored to the slip. James Fitzmaurice had said it was a neat harbor, but Pat knew that it had only seemed so after the wild and terrible sea outside.

In the morning, when he reached the slip, he would not
have been surprised to find the hooker gone. But she was
there, lying in against the low shelter of the slip like a pup
crouching against a house door on a wet night. She was high
and dry, because the tide was low. The reef was bare, all
except the tip which was catching the incoming waves and
sending them shooting upwards. Patches of white showed
here and there among the heavy black clouds. The shore was
white with sea gulls, wailing dismally to each other as they
profited from the low tide to pick up their breakfast. A few
hardier ones were climbing the tall waves outside, perhaps
hoping for an unlucky fish.

Mike was already at the slip.

"Your father was right," he said. "This will be a better
day. She's a grand boat."

She was indeed a grand boat, shaped like the body of a
bird to ride the waves. Her mast was a larch tree, still new
enough to show the marks of the adze with which it had
been shaped. All her ropes were fairly new too, and her
sails were not yet faded by the salty winds and spray.

"She's all shipshape," Pat said. "She's a well-thought-of
boat."

She had even been freshly tarred, and her name, *Naomh
Éinde*, was painted on her bows in small white letters.

"That name probably means she's an Aran boat," said
Mike. "Naomh Éinde is the Aran saint. Was the stranger
out of bed when you left home?"

"He was. He was starting on his breakfast but he didn't
seem to have much mind for it. I hadn't much mind for
mine either." He paused for a moment and then said,
"Mike, are you afraid?"

"Yes," Mike said, "but I suppose the men waiting for an

ambush are often afraid too. It would only be a queer person that wouldn't be afraid."

"We'll get there safely."

"We will, I think. If we can get out on the half-tide we'll be over by nightfall. On a day like this, no one will be watching the sea for boats."

"There's another reason why we can go safely," said Pat. "I'm a Conneeley, and the Conneeleys can't be drowned."

"You don't believe that old story, surely!"

"I do believe it," Pat said hotly. "My father said it. You heard him. The breed of the seal is in us. We can't be drowned. So the boat must go safe."

"Maybe you should fill up the boat with Conneeleys so."

"If I could find enough of them I would," Pat said angrily.

Mike said quickly:

"I'm not afraid. I'm going with you. I promised last night, sitting in your own kitchen. I was only joking you about the seals. How do we know what old story is behind that belief? Maybe the seals did save a Conneeley man from drowning, in some long-ago time."

"My father doesn't believe that story," Pat said. "If he did, he wouldn't have refused to sail over to Connemara today."

"He didn't exactly refuse," said Mike. "He just said that if he set off in the hooker, he wouldn't get beyond the reef. The way it is with people when they get older, they get careful. They don't feel like walking on the cliffs on a windy day, nor going down the face of the cliff after the puffins' eggs, nor climbing up the mast of a hooker, nor walking along the roof when the thatching is being done. I think their bones get a bit stiff, especially in their feet. And they seem to see things we don't see at all, waiting to trip them up."

"Maybe so," Pat said. "But I'm not sorry we won't have any older people with us this time, to be warning us of the dangers."

He seemed so satisfied with this that Mike said no more about it, though he knew that a danger can often be avoided if the warning comes in time. Besides, he thought, James Fitzmaurice had come alone from Lettermore, and two boys might possibly equal one man in wisdom and skill and experience. He said as much to Pat.

"Three boys," Pat said.

"Three? Who is the third?"

"Jerry Lynskey."

"Why?"

"To stop the talk. Did you hear it last night? Did you hear my grandfather telling that old story as if it only happened last week? Jerry will have that story tied to him forever, like a block of wood around the neck of a wandering sheepdog. It's no wonder Owen Lynskey is always talking about the old gods and the old heroes, to try to take the people's minds off the history of his own family. And no wonder he's frightened-looking and shiftless. How could he have any respect for himself, knowing that that story is in everyone's mouth? If Jerry comes with us now, there will be a hero in the Lynskey family for a change."

"But do you think he has the courage——"

"You see," said Pat, "you have the same idea yourself. We're all our lives looking at Jerry and we don't rightly know what he's like. If he comes with us, we'll know a lot more. He hardly ever says what's in his mind, only stays quiet and listens to other people talking. Have you noticed that?"

"I have," said Mike, "and I remember my father saying once that Jerry was the makings of a fine man, if he got a chance."

"Come on, then, and we'll ask him to sail with us," said Pat.

chapter 4

A Plan

As they went up the hill, there were few people to be seen. In the small fields, the little oats and barley that was grown on the island was being blown out flat by the wind. No man would want to watch while the labor of the spring was destroyed, so they all found work to do inside their houses—mending nets and lobster pots and tools, or even writing letters to their relations in America. Maggie had said once, as she settled down with her penny pen and her bottle of ink:

"The people over there must think there's a storm all the time in the islands. Every letter of mine begins the same way—'As I take up my pen to write to you, the wind is blowing strong from the west and we're expecting a mighty storm.' "

On this morning, the cattle were sheltering under the

walls and the hens were huddled on their perches. Even there, the wind was catching their feathers and blowing them until they showed pale. The donkeys had pushed their way into the cart-sheds and were standing inside, staring angrily with their long ears poked forward. Only the goats seemed unconcerned. They were making the most of their chances, now that there was no one to watch them, nipping into cabbage patches and flower gardens wherever the gaps in the walls were low enough.

At Lynskeys', the boys saw that the Connors' big billy goat was working along the only line of cabbages in the field beside the house. Furiously they chased him out, pelting him with stones as he galloped down the road. While they were at this, Jerry Lynskey came out of the house. Pat and Mike ran back, panting, to where Jerry was sadly examining the damage.

"He got enough to give him a fine stomachache, anyway," said Jerry, "if that's any satisfaction. Thanks for chasing him."

"We must mend the gap," Pat said. "That's how he got in, the villain."

They brought big stones and some thorny branches to fill the gap. When they had finished, Mike said:

"And the Connors will have to give you some heads of cabbage to make up for what the billy goat took. They won't mind doing that—they have plenty, and they're always decent when they have it."

"I know," Jerry said. "But I'd be ashamed to ask them; they have given us so much already. Anyway I should have kept a watch on that gap myself."

He stopped, but the others knew what he had been thinking—that it was his father's business to see to the walls and gaps, but that he had neglected them as usual.

"It's a good job you happened to be passing," Jerry said.

"We weren't just passing—we came to get you. Come on away up the hill to the cave and we'll be talking."

They raced each other up the hill, at every step pushing against the wind as if it were a great, soft, invisible wall. The road ran over the hilltop and down toward the sea again, but after a while it became just a grassy track. This was because no one lived at that side of the island. There was no shelter there from the west wind and it was more sensible to build at the other side of the hill where at least the greatest strength of the wind was broken.

Only the lightkeepers had their lonely tower down there among the waves and the spray. In bad weather they were imprisoned there, with nothing to do all day long but read or watch the sea birds. Some of them were great readers, and it was said too that they often found strange birds after a storm and sent them off to Dublin to be examined by experts.

Looking down from the highest point of the island, the boys saw the huge, gray-green, terrifying sea, speckled with white, stretching away and away to the other side of the world. They gave it no more than a glance before turning off to the left, where a track led a little way down to a tumble of gray rocks.

Here there were several caves, with their openings turned conveniently away from the wind. The bigger ones were full of sheltering sheep and their half-grown lambs. The boys knew better than to go near them, not only because of the stench that hung around them but also because they harbored a specially nasty, fat tick which would as soon feed on a boy as on a sheep, and which for all its girth had a very long spring.

Instead they went to the cave they called their own. Its entrance was so narrow that only a lamb could have fitted through it, and these usually stayed with their mothers until they were too fat to get in. Therefore the floor was clean inside, and the boys had brought an old brush to keep it so. There were a few old creepie stools, past mending and given up reluctantly by Maggie after long persuasion. Best of all, there was a little hearthstone with a hole cut out of the soft rock above it to serve as a chimney. This had been done by someone in the bad old times, Jim Conneeley said, to make a hiding place where a man could live in safety for months together if he were careful about the times of lighting his fire.

Inside the cave, it was suddenly very quiet. They heard only a faint moaning sound now, because the roof was thickly covered in grass and earth.

"We'll make a fire first," Pat said, "and then we can talk."

He loved to make a fire, even if they knew they would only be an hour in the cave. They always kept a little stack of turf there. They broke off the soft feathery outside pieces of the sods to use as kindling. When these were well alight, they surrounded them with harder pieces, slightly bigger. Gradually the fire grew until they had a little volcano blazing away on the hearthstone.

"I can always feel my brains working better when there's a fire," Pat said. He paused, wondering whether Jerry would be insulted at what he was going to say. But there was no way out. "Before I tell you why we came for you, we'll have to warn you that it's dangerous. If you'd rather not be in it, you can just say so now and then we won't bother with telling you the whole story at all."

"I don't mind the danger, if it's something to do with the war," Jerry said. Then he said easily, "And even if I knew your story, I wouldn't lay information about it."

"There was no need to say that," Pat said.

"There was need," said Jerry. "Everyone stops talking about the war as soon as I come along, or my father. He doesn't mind. He says it's always like that when you have an informer in the family, and it's no good fighting it. He says every Lynskey in Connemara has a black mark on him, from my great-grandfather."

Pat and Mike were astonished at this speech. They had never before heard Jerry say so much. And it was all said so clearly and calmly, it was more like the talk of a grown man than of a boy.

"You've done a bit of thinking," Pat said at last.

"I have plenty of time for it," said Jerry. "I suppose you're going to tell me something about the wounded man that came on the hooker alone, late last night."

"How do you know about him?"

"I helped him to land." He laughed at their amazed expressions. "He needed help. He could never have managed it alone, with only one arm working."

James Fitzmaurice had mentioned a boy who had helped him, but they had been so much excited that they had forgotten this part of the story. Mike asked:

"How did you know he was coming?"

"I saw the light on his masthead. I saw it from the field behind our own house when I went out to have a look at the weather. I didn't like to call anyone out on such a bad night for fear they'd say I was only imagining it. So I just went down to the slip myself."

Pat remembered how he had thought the hooker was a ghost ship and had immediately skipped into the house.

"You went down to the slip alone?"

"Yes. I could have asked my father to go with me but he doesn't like to be out on a bad night either. When I got down there, the hooker was just coming in to the slip. He had the sails down, but they were in a big heap and he couldn't have got them tidied up by himself. He threw me a rope and I moored the boat, and then I helped to put away the sails. I walked up the hill with him and showed him your father's house in the distance."

"He wants someone to sail over to Lettermore in his boat

to fetch my uncle," Pat said. "My father said the weather is too bad now. He said the boat wouldn't get outside the reef. He said he'll go when the storm is over, but that might be too late."

"So what are you thinking of?"

"Yesterday," said Pat, "my father told us that the storm will ease off today and blow up again tomorrow. He's always right about storms. It's a little quieter today."

"It's an ugly sea."

"Yes, but it was worse yesterday. That looks a good boat."

"She sails like a swan. But it's seven miles to Lettermore."

"First we'll have shelter from the island and then we'll have shelter from the mainland. I often heard the men say it. Only the middle part is bad."

"Maybe we won't get there at all."

"Maybe. But we're going to try. If you don't want to come——"

"I want to come. It's just that I like to see what's in front of me."

"I'd rather not see."

"That's the way I'm made," said Jerry. "I don't like to be surprised. There's plenty of people that like it better your way. How soon are we going?"

"As soon as the hooker is afloat. That will be at the half-tide. The wind might lighten a bit then. We should be over in four or five hours."

As he said this, Pat could feel a great shudder go through him, as if he were already on the plunging hooker being blown across the wild dark sea. They were all silent for a few minutes. Then Mike said:

"I see no way out of it. And it's no use sailing there until we have a boat under us, at least. We have plenty of things to think about besides a lot of misfortunes that might never happen."

Pat remembered the marvelous lines that the teacher, Michael Cooney, had read for them at school, just before it closed for the summer:

> Cowards die many times before their death.
> The valiant never taste of death but once.

Now the teacher had gone away, and he had said that he would not be back to work until the war was over. He had left exact instructions to the older boys about running the school in his absence, especially about teaching the smaller boys to read. He had not said where he was going but everyone had guessed that he was going to join his brigade in Clifden.

Planning some food to bring along made them all more cheerful, as if it were going to be an excursion for fun. Jerry said:

"I can bring a few eggs."

"And I'll get a loaf of bread," said Pat. "My mother was making two this morning."

"Our potatoes will be boiled by the time I get home," said Mike. "I'll get a little potful, and a couple of bottles of water."

"We'll have to be careful," said Jerry. "If we're seen making for the slip with those things, the whole island will be out to stop us."

Pat said:

"James Fitzmaurice will help us, of course. We'd better go and find him."

They extinguished the remains of their fire, and then went

outside. At once they saw that while they had been in the cave a tiny patch of blue had appeared in the sky. Around it the black and gray clouds still spun and circled, but the day had brightened a little. The sea was rolling more evenly, though the waves were as big as ever. Now that their shape could be seen, they were no longer quite so terrifying.

They guessed that James Fitzmaurice would be at the slip, and they started for it at once. From the top of the hill they saw that a little crowd had gathered there.

"Of course there's a crowd," said Pat. "By this time everyone must know the hooker is here. We'll go down anyway, and I'll try to get him to come away and talk to us."

Jerry hung back saying:

"Perhaps I'd better stay here."

Pat hesitated too. It was true that since all the islanders would have guessed at once that James Fitzmaurice was on the run, they would be uneasy at the presence of a Lynskey among them. Still he said:

"It's time there was an end of all that nonsense. You come with us and don't mind what anyone says."

"They never say anything to me," said Jerry. "They just think it."

At the top of the slip they slowed down. Edging through the crowd, they saw that the men gathered there did indeed throw uneasy glances at Jerry. Pat and Mike noticed too how Jerry seemed to have developed a trick of going very still, obviously to avoid attention. He never looked directly at anyone and he kept always rather to the outside of the little crowd of people.

Old John Faherty was there with Morgan Conneeley. Everyone was discussing the same thing, whether the boat would be safe at the slip until the storm would die down. It was not a very useful kind of argument, as Morgan said:

"We could try to sail her around into the long harbor but we might lose her on the way there. What good would that do us or her?"

"No good at all," everyone agreed.

Pat kept very quiet, listening to this. The long harbor was not a real harbor at all but a sort of narrow slit in the rocky cliff to the other side of the reef. No matter how fierce the storm might be, inside it was always perfectly calm and still. This was because the waves broke outside, against an outcropping rock, which made entry into the long harbor very difficult at any time and almost impossible during a storm. The island hookers were always kept there, for this reason. If the men decided to bring the strange boat in there now, there would be no hope at all of getting her out again.

Pat shouldered his way gently through the crowd until he was standing at the very front of it, beside James Fitzmaurice. The islandmen were doing all the talking. James was watching them tiredly, turning to look at each one as he spoke. Pat pulled silently at his sleeve. When James turned slowly to look down at him, he just gave one jerk with his head. Then he pushed his way out of the crowd again.

In a moment, sure enough he saw that James was following him. Mike and Jerry were coming over too. Slowly Pat moved off, as if to get a better view of the slip from the side. The others followed, and there they stood, in view of everyone but too far away to be heard.

Pat said at once:

"The three of us will sail your boat to Lettermore for you."

James did not show any sign of surprise. He just seemed suddenly to become more alive. He said:

"Have you sailed before? Alone?"

"Never alone, but we've all sailed."

"In bad weather?"

"Never as bad as this."

"It's dangerous."

"We know. But with three of us it should be all right."

"You think the men won't go?"

"Never. I can tell by their talk."

"Why are they so much afraid?"

"They're not afraid. They're just sensible."

"You couldn't go alone. If you could find one man, even, that would go with you——"

He paused, and they watched him. It was impossible to tell what he was thinking. Then he said:

"If I let you go off in my hooker to Lettermore, I might turn everyone on the island against the whole movement. Perhaps I should go with you myself."

"That's not what you planned," said Mike.

"No, but one must always be ready to change the plan."

"I can think of one man who might go with us," said Pat.

"He'd need to be independent—a man that wouldn't mind what the neighbors would say to him afterwards."

"He never cares what the neighbors say, so long as he knows he's doing right. A short while ago he told me that being old doesn't matter to him, because he still feels about twelve years old inside."

"Who is this man?"

"My grandfather," said Pat. "Morgan Conneeley."

chapter 5

A Line
of Seals

"Morgan Conneeley?" said James. "Will he be lively enough, at his age?"

"You should see him roll up a bolt of cloth and shoot it up on the shelf. You should see him——"

"How is he in a boat?"

"He hasn't sailed for years alone, but when he was young he won the race from the island to Carraroe so many times that they were going to give up having it at all, my father told me, if he wouldn't stay out of it."

"To Carraroe? Then he knows the coast well?"

"Like the back of his hand."

"Go over and fetch him, then," said James. "There's no time to lose."

While they had been talking, the clouds had blown higher. They rolled and tumbled over each other still but they were a lighter color now than they had been in the morning. This had made the sea's color change to an emerald green. They could not see the mainland for the clouds of mist that hung over the sea. The wind had shifted a point to the north and was steadier now, but colder.

Everything showed that the sooner they got under way, the more chance they would have of a safe passage. Now that the time had come, Pat found that he dared not think closely of what they were going to do. His skin prickled all over with a special kind of alertness so that he felt as if he had suddenly grown bigger and stronger.

When Pat reached him, his grandfather was standing with Jim and old John Faherty on the very edge of the slip, looking down into the boat. Everyone else had moved back, to escape the flying tips of the waves which were continually spraying over the slip like a shower of rain. The hooker rose and fell easily on the swell, riding it like a bird.

"She's a grand boat," Morgan was saying. "If one man would come with me now, I'd sail her over myself."

Jim Conneeley said:

"Don't you know I'd go with you, Father, if I didn't know it's madness? What's the good of losing the boat and drowning ourselves? Then we'd never get Roddy out of Lettermore at all. You said yourself only a minute ago that that would be foolishness."

"Did I say that?" said Morgan.

Jim turned away to talk to old John Faherty and get his agreement. Pat slipped in beside Morgan and said:

"James Fitzmaurice wants to talk to you."

Instantly Morgan came with him. No one took any notice of them. Probably the people were thinking that the old man was heartbroken over the danger to his son in Lettermore, and the fact that he could not go to help him. They would have been glad to have seen him leave the slip, where the presence of the boat would be a torment to him.

As they went across to where James was standing, Morgan said again:

"If I could get one man to go with me, I'd sail her over myself."

Pat said:

"I heard my father say that you think it can't be done."

"I didn't say that. I said that we couldn't put the hooker into the long harbor. That's because we wouldn't get her safe around the reef, barring a miracle. If I were going to Lettermore, I wouldn't go near the reef. I'd go north first, into the wind. Then when I'd be outside the level of the reef, I'd steer for Lettermore. It's a big sea, but I've seen bigger."

By this time they had reached the others. James said to Pat, "Have you told him? Does he agree?"

"I haven't told him yet but I think he'll do all right."

"What's this? What are you saying?" Morgan asked excitedly.

"The boys say they could take the boat over to Lettermore for Roddy," said James. "It's a fine offer, but I can't let them go alone. Will you go with them?"

"Thanks be to God!" said old Morgan. "We're still rearing men. It's not that our men are afraid, you must understand that. It's just that they know it can't be done. And they think we can wait. If they saw a boat drowning out there, they'd be out in their dozens to save it. But this time they think there's no hurry for a couple of days."

"There isn't a moment to lose," said James. "This clearer spell may last for a few hours. With God's help it will be enough to get you over and back. Do you know the Folans' house at Lettermore? Simon Folan's, that is, right by the quay?"

"Of course I do. Many a night I spent there, yarning and chatting until the dawn of day. Is old Matthew alive still?"

"He is, and kicking. How long is it since you were there?"

"It's ten years and more. Of course I hear tell of them now and then but I haven't heard of Matthew for a while. A queer thing happens when you get old; people don't want to be telling you when other old people die. How soon can we go?"

"At once, this moment."

"In front of all the people?"

"Why not?"

"Wouldn't it be better to wait until they go home to their dinner?"

"If you wait, the wind might change again. They won't stop you if you can go fast enough. There's oilskins in plenty on the boat, and dry jerseys, and food and water. The food isn't very fancy but it's enough to keep you alive. There are guns there too. Have you ever used one?"

"I have, after foxes and rabbits," Morgan said.

"Don't use the guns if you don't have to. I'd like everything to be very quiet. The shots would be heard a long way off and besides we have no ammunition to spare. Now we'll walk back slowly to the boat. We'll go to the edge of the slip—you see, they're drifting away from it already."

It was true that the people had scattered a little. One or two had begun to go up the hill to their homes. The rest were still talking eagerly to each other but they were no longer gathered so closely. It almost seemed as if they were not talking so much of the boat and its owner as of the storm. James said:

"When I'm ready, I'll count three. At the third you can all jump on board. I'll have her cast off before anyone can come near."

Without appearing to hurry, they all walked back toward the slip. Old John Faherty stepped forward and caught Morgan by the arm.

"Let you come home with me, Morgan," he said. "There's no more to be done. In a few days the boat will go over. Come home with me now and don't be tormenting yourself any more."

"One look only," said Morgan. "I'll be with you later."

John Faherty dropped his arm, mystified at the cheerful note in his old friend's voice. He stood watching them while they continued on their way to the slip.

By the time they were alongside the hooker, they were aware that everyone else had turned to look at them too. Pat wanted to spring on board at once, if only to get free of all those watching eyes. It seemed as if the people had sensed that something strange was about to happen. It was an agony to wait while James said softly:

"When you get to Lettermore, don't delay for anything less than a hurricane. Roddy will be expecting you. If something goes wrong and you have to separate, try to go in pairs. At least one of each pair should live to tell the tale." He grinned at them cheerfully though his words were grim. Then he said, "In a moment I'm going to start counting."

With a casual air he walked to the first bollard. His voice came to them from there, counting. At the third they all stepped aboard the hooker. Old Morgan was the first, so light he seemed almost to be dancing. He picked up the boat hook. At the bollard James flipped the rope free. By now all the men had seen what was happening. A murmur went up from them and one or two ran forward. Swiftly

James moved to the second bollard. Already the bows of the
hooker were away from the ship. Under instructions from
Morgan, the boys were hauling up sail. The old man was at
the helm now. James sent the second rope flying through
the air.

At once it seemed as if the hooker had been seized by a
huge hand and twisted around. She made a great sweeping
curve with the wind roaring in her canvas. The noise of it
was so loud that the shout that had gone up from the men
on shore seemed ridiculously light and high, almost like the
cry of the sea gulls. They looked back for a moment and

saw James Fitzmaurice waving his good arm. Then the men
gathered in around him and there was no time to watch any
more.

The hooker was tearing along at a frightening speed. The
long creaking sound of her timbers was comfortable, however. She climbed each wave with a confident air and she
did not shiver as she plunged downward. Not a drop of
water came aboard. Often Pat had heard the men discussing the design of their hookers, saying how perfect they
were in a heavy sea. It was the inward curve of the gun-
whale that saved them from being splashed by every wave,
so that they never shipped any water.

Already the island looked small and very far away. On
their port side, a hideous welter of water foamed around the
reef. The speed of the waves seemed faster over there. Old
Morgan kept well out from it, as he had said he would do.
Pat thought that if they had been even a few yards nearer, it
would have sucked the hooker into its jaws and chewed it
up.

But they were giving the reef a wide berth. Soon it was

far astern. They were heading north, almost into the wind.
Pat glanced at his grandfather, who was standing at the helm
as straight as the mast. Trimming the sails in that wind was
a task that took every moment of the boys' attention, but
Pat had time to notice that the old man looked as con-
tented as when he stood at the loom. They had not been
many minutes at sea before he realized that it would have
been madness indeed to have gone without him.

A quarter of a mile offshore, they came about and began
to sail before the wind for Lettermore. Now they were so
far beyond the tip of the reef that it seemed almost harm-
less when they passed it. Pat went and stood beside his
grandfather.

"My father will be furious with us when we get back," he
said.

"He won't, faith," said old Morgan. "I'll tell you how it
will be. If we get back safe with Roddy, he'll have to admit
we were right to go. If we were right, why should he be
angry? On the other side of the story, if we don't get back
safe and sound, he'll be so busy lamenting for us that he
won't have time to be angry, and even if he gets angry, it
won't affect us because we won't be there."

This made a kind of sense, though the second part of it
was not very cheerful. Old Morgan added:

"Coming back will be harder, if the wind stays in the
north. If it goes more westerly, it will blow stronger and
that will be worse."

But he looked so pleased that Pat asked in astonishment:

"Then why aren't you afraid?"

"You're only afraid before you do a thing," Morgan explained. "And sometimes you're afraid after you've done it.
But never while you're doing it. That's how it is with me.

And there's another thing. I was in the Fenian Brotherhood
when I was in Boston and I never got a chance to strike a
blow for my country. There were some went over from
there to Australia and rescued some Fenians that were in
one of the terrible prisons there. I used to pray that some-

thing like that would come again before I'd die, and now here it is. It's well for you, to have this piece of luck and you only a young lad."

They found the food in a locker by the helm. It was cooked salt bacon, very fatty, and a week-old loaf of soda-bread, hard as a rock. Pat thought wryly of the fresh loaf and the hard-boiled eggs that they had planned to bring. Now it struck him suddenly that even if there had been no food aboard, James would not have allowed them to delay long enough to fetch some. They would have had to live hungrily until they reached Lettermore. Even there, there might be no time to stop and eat. This thought sharpened his appetite so that the queer food went down like a king's banquet.

They had hardly finished eating when the sea and the wind seemed suddenly to grow fiercer. They had moved out of the shelter of the island and now the wind came at them wickedly, as if it wanted to force the hooker under. Still she climbed those terrible waves, almost as though she were moving forward to meet them. One would think she was en-joying her wrestling match with them, especially when every eighth or ninth wave seemed to change its rhythm in a wily effort to get the better of her. But she was at her ease, even in a sea like this.

"She's a grand boat," said Morgan. "I'd sail her to Amer-ica, so I would."

"That's what I'd like to do when I grow up," said Mike. "I'd take this very boat, and I'd never stop till I'd crossed the Atlantic Ocean."

"Why?" Morgan asked.

"I don't know. I just want to."

"I'd only go for a good reason," said Jerry.

Morgan laughed. "It should be the other way around," he said. "Jerry's father is a dreamy man, always talking about the long voyages the old heroes made, to the well at the world's end and to the Islands of Greece after golden apples that were always like new, and to the court of the King of the Western World. Mike's father, the light of heaven to his soul, was the exact opposite. He had to have a reason for doing everything. He was a great planner. He was always ahead of everyone else with his planting and his lobsters. He'd be the first down on the shore collecting the seaweed after a storm. Even his cattle were fat before everyone else's. It would be more fitting for Mike to be like him."

"That's what my mother says," said Mike. "She doesn't like me to go to sea, even in a currach."

Pat knew that this was true. Mrs. Hernon hated to see Mike go fishing or swimming with the other boys. He wondered how she was feeling now. She had not been at the slip, but long before this some neighbor would surely have told her that her son had gone off on the strange hooker with the weaver and two other boys. One good thing was that she would never stop praying for their safety until they reached home again.

Deep among the waves as they were, they could see no trace of the mainland. The island had disappeared too, so that it seemed almost as if Mike were having his wish and they were really on their way across the Atlantic Ocean. It was a lonesome feeling, and Pat found himself glad of the company of the sea gulls that were following in their wake. They dipped and dived and sailed over the waves, sometimes disappearing under water and coming up with a twitching fish. He noticed that they always seized only fish of the right size—neither too big nor too small. Sometimes the men found little fat sharks in the nets, and he wondered what would happen if a sea gull were to seize one of those by mistake.

It seemed a long time before they felt the shelter of the mainland. When it came, they were as pleased as if the storm had suddenly died down. Still the waves were long gray monsters, peering in at them with hungry curiosity.

Ahead of them, the rocky shore was white with foam, it seemed along its whole length.

For the first time, Morgan looked troubled. He gave a little nervous laugh and said:

"How are we to see the channel in a sea like this? I've sailed it so often, I could do it blindfold, but all the same I'd like to see the marks. Can any of you see them?"

"What do they look like?"

"Little white towers to port, black to starboard."

"How could anyone see black or white today?"

"Ah, well, I'll find it as I often found it before," said Morgan, but he did not look satisfied.

It was then that Pat saw the line of seals. Afterward he could never understand how he had seen them at all in the churning water. Only their heads showed, round and bald

like babies, but black all over. A streak of sunlight touched them, and perhaps that was why he noticed them. He pulled at his grandfather's sleeve and said:

"Look! There go our cousins. If we could whistle to them, maybe they'd lead us in to the quay."

Morgan looked where Pat was pointing. The seals were quite near. There were six or seven of them, swimming quickly toward the shore, but crossing the hooker's course at an angle of forty-five degrees.

"We don't need to whistle," said Morgan. "They'll be making for the calm water near the quay, for certain sure. They don't like rough water. We only have to follow them."

He brought the hooker about. The speed of the seals astonished Pat. They had been well ahead of the hooker when he had seen them first and they were easily able to keep pace with it. He wished he could see their little anxious faces with the drooping mustaches, but they were too far away and too low in the water. Morgan said:

"What in the name of all that's wonderful brought them out in the storm? It's our luck—we were off our course until we saw them. There's the quay ahead of us."

"Maybe they knew there was a boatload of Conneeleys coming," said Pat.

"Maybe," said Morgan. "Those seals came at the right moment, anyway."

Very soon afterward they were sliding in to the little stone quay. Jerry and Mike sprang ashore and made the hooker fast. The others followed, and they all started up the quay. Not one of them turned to look back at the sea.

chapter 6

~~~~~~~~~~~~~~~~~~~~~~~~~~~~~~~~~~

A Journey
on Horseback

Folan's house was the one nearest
to the sea, James Fitzmaurice had said. They saw it at once,
with its front door shut fast against the wind. An old fishing
net had been pegged over its thatch to prevent it from
blowing away during a storm. The front walls were covered
with pink cabbage roses, which managed to cling on in spite
of the wind. There were wallflowers there too, but they had
been skinned by the same salty wind. The earth underneath
them was red with their petals.

Inside the house, a dog barked.

"We'd better go in," said Morgan. "That fellow will
warn half the neighborhood."

They moved toward the gable of the house, but before
they could reach it a man appeared there. He took a step

forward eagerly when he saw them and then stopped, disappointed. Morgan said:

"Simon Folan?"

"That's my name," said the man, trying at once to look hospitable. "And who may you be?"

"Morgan Conneeley from the island."

The man's face lit up. "You're Roddy's father. It's a long time since you were here."

"It is, so. Is Roddy here?"

"He hasn't come yet. I thought it was himself, when Shep barked. We'd better go inside."

He led the way around the end of the house to the back door. It was standing open, because it was sheltered from the wind.

From his place beside the fire, the dog growled gently when they came in. An old man who was sitting on the hob beside him said softly:

"Quiet, Shep. That's enough out of you."

Morgan went across quickly to greet his old friend.

"And Matthew, old stock, how are you doing?"

Pat watched while they thumped each other and laughed with pleasure at meeting again. Simon said:

"He's here in good time for taking Roddy away."

"When did you expect him?" Morgan asked.

A woman came out of the inner room.

"Last night he should have been here," she said and her voice was full of terror. "God knows what has happened to him. We've had no word, and there's those scoundrels going around like walking devils, killing and murdering all around them——"

"Easy on, Nora," said Simon. "That sort of talk doesn't do any good."

"He should have been here last night?" Morgan said.

Simon shrugged. "It was a terrible night. And who's going to say when anyone will come in times like these?"

"What way would he come?"

"If it was calmer weather, I'd say he might have come by sea, but in weather like this he must come by the Cois Fhairrge road, or else over the mountains."

"Which would be more likely?"

"Cois Fhairrge, of course." Simon talked very energetically, so that everything he said almost seemed like an insult. "That's the straight road by the sea as far as Carraroe, then over to Casla and out here to Lettermore. He knows every stone on the way."

"Where would he stop, if he had to stop?"

"At Knock, maybe, or Rossaveel, or even in Carraroe. But I'm thinking that if he got to Carraroe, he'd be able to send over someone to tell us he's safe."

There was a pause for a moment after Simon had said this, while they all thought of the possible reasons why no message had come. Pat found that all the breath had left his lungs. He was bending stiffly forward, looking eagerly from one face to another as the men spoke, while a certain thought grew and grew in his head. At last he could hold it in no longer. The words tumbled stutteringly out of him:

"Can you get me a horse?"

They all looked at him in surprise that a boy should speak while such serious matters were being discussed by his elders.

Then Simon said:

"I have a horse. I thought of going down to find him, but a man on a horse would be sure to be stopped."

"A boy on a horse would get through," said Pat.

"A boy?"

"I'll go. You can tell me where to look for him. One of

the others can come with me. James Fitzmaurice said that
if we have to separate, we should go in pairs."

"I'll come with you," said Jerry.

Now the men were looking at them with delight. Morgan
said:

"Yes, yes, you can go, and myself and Mike will have the
boat ready to sail the moment you come back."

"While they're gone, you can wait here with us," said old
Matthew. "We can be telling you all the news of the country, and bad news it is."

"When I was asking what road he'd come," said Morgan,
"I was thinking of going myself to look for him. A man on a
horse would be stopped, you said, but when you're my age
you're hardly counted a man at all."

"You're counted a man as long as you can sail over from
the islands on a day like this," said Simon. "Come away out
and we'll saddle the horse."

"Wait, wait," said Nora. "They can't go empty. Do you
want them to fall off the horse with starvation? You must
give me time to get something ready for them. What did
you eat on the boat?" she asked Pat.

"There was bread and bacon," he said.

"I know by the way you said it that it wouldn't put much
heart in you. I'll cook something better for you now while
you're out getting to know the horse."

They left her flying around the kitchen. The whole company went outside. In the field beside the house, the horse
lifted his head at once to look at them, with his ears poked
forward. He was a slim bay, very tall, and with big, intelli-
gent eyes. Matthew Folan went over to the wall.

"Come on over here, horse, till we give you your orders,"
he said.

The horse came over and pushed at him with his nose. Pat and Jerry reached up and stroked it.

"I'd get fond of that horse," said Pat.

Jerry said, "So would I. How will he like carrying the two of us?"

"No bother at all," said Simon. "Often he carries myself and Nora, though she doesn't like it much. Two boys will be easy for him."

He opened the gate and led the horse out of the field.

"He's a young horse," he said. "Only three years old. If we'd had the races this year, he'd have won all before him. But they wouldn't let us have the races for fear that when we'd get together we'd be plotting, and that's just what we'd be doing. Do you know what Roddy has been at?" he asked sharply.

"There was to be an ambush at Oranmore."

"Yes. Now, you'd better forget you ever heard that. You're two brothers from Mweenish and you're on your way to stay with your aunt in Knock. She's your mother's sister, a Mrs. Curran. If anyone stops you, you can ask for directions to get to her house—it's a few years since you've been to visit her and you're not quite sure where it is. A great thing, if you're held up and questioned, is to ask a few questions yourself first. Mrs. Curran is a widow, so she can't leave home to visit her sister. Now tell me all that back again."

"We're brothers," said Pat, and he looked sideways at Jerry. It was strange to have a brother.

"When you say it, don't look at him," said Simon. "Begin again."

"This is my brother," Pat said boldly. "We're going to Knock, to visit our aunt, our mother's sister. She's a widow so she can't come to visit us. She has no one to mind the chickens and the pigs for her. So our mother said that though the times are dangerous we'd better take the horse and go down to see is she all right and maybe do a few jobs for her."

"Good man," Simon said. "That's the way to do it. You'd better keep your own names. What are they? Pat and Jerry? It would be dangerous to change them. You might make a mistake."

He led the horse to the back door and took the saddle from its peg in the kitchen.

"Saddle him yourself," he said to Pat. "That's how you'll get to know him."

But it took both boys to saddle him, he was so tall. When they had tightened the girths, Simon tested them to make sure that they had been done strongly enough.

"That's well done," he said. "Nothing a horse hates so much as a loose girth. You'll have to unsaddle him on the way, if you stop the night somewhere."

They slipped off the headstall over the horse's ears and put on his bridle. He stroked the ground once with his right front hoof.

"He's anxious to be off," old Matthew said. "He's had no exercise for a week. That fellow would carry you to Galway and back without any bother, forty miles each way."

By this time, a wonderful smell of frying bacon was filling the kitchen and drifting out into the yard. Nora called them, and they found great plates of bacon and eggs waiting, and strong tea. She had cut a mountain of soda-bread and she seemed to want them to get it all inside them before they left the house. When they could not, she made sandwiches with more bacon and wrapped them up in a cloth, to be brought with them.

When they were mounted one behind the other on the horse, Simon said:

"That story about your aunt, Mrs. Curran, will do for anyone that asks you. Knock is the next village after the lake. Mrs. Curran won't be surprised to see you. Whoever comes to her door can be her cousin or her nephew or her brother-in-law. She's not a bit particular. Her house is the second one you'll see, well up off the road on the left-hand side. As you go along, you'll have to talk to people, and if they're friendly, you can ask about Roddy. We've had no news of the ambush out here in the back of beyond, but we'll be getting it today for sure. You will be getting news of it too, so that when you come back we can put our stories together."

"How will we know if the people are friendly?"

"Any house where the door stands open is friendly," old Matthew said. "When you go to the door, if the woman brings you in and makes tea for you, that will be a sign of a friendly house. If you're still not sure, and if you're going away without asking any questions, and she says: 'God speed you, God's blessing go with you,' then you can turn back and talk to her. But if you see the door shut, and a clipped hedge in front, and a little brass knocker that you'd be supposed to bang on the door with before they'd let you in, then you should keep away from that house as if the devil were inside in it. But there aren't many houses like that on the road between this and Galway."

"Off with ye," said Simon, "and use the brains God gave ye."

He tapped the horse to make him move. At once he walked quickly out of the yard and down the laneway that led to the road. The voices of the little crowd that was left behind came after them on the wind:

"God speed ye!"

"Safe journey!"

"God's blessing go with ye!"

Out on the road, Pat shook the reins and the horse broke into a trot. It was a big saddle and they sat in it comfortably together, Pat in front holding the reins and Jerry with a light hold on the back of Pat's jersey. When Nora traveled with her husband, she would have sat sideways, far back. It was no wonder she did not care for this way of traveling.

Once they were away from the house, the wind seemed to want to lift them both off the horse and carry them away over the mountains. They were so high that they could see over the stone walls at their right side, all the way down to the tossing gray and white sea. The dust of the road whirled around them, kicked up by the horse's hoofs. The clouds were still high and white, crossing and recrossing the sky as if the wind up there were blowing in every direction at once.

Pat remembered uneasily what his father had said about the storm, that it would probably slacken off that day and blow up again the next. Already most of the day was gone. It would be light until ten o'clock and twilight for half an hour after that. Then, with those heavy clouds, there would be the blackest darkness.

"How far can we go in three or four hours, I wonder," he said. "It must be seven o'clock now."

"I was thinking of the same thing," said Jerry. "We'll get as far as Knock easily enough, before dark. Maybe we won't have to go that far. Maybe we'll hear some news of him before that."

"I hope my father is wrong, for once," said Pat. "If the storm holds off until tomorrow evening——"

But so many things could happen before tomorrow evening that they did not want to think about it.

The horse was certainly enjoying his outing. He seemed to be not at all concerned about the weather. The only sign of annoyance he showed was by twitching his ears sometimes when a strong gust of wind struck him. Mile after mile he trotted along, keeping to the grassy verge of the road. Once when they passed by another horse in a field, he lifted his head and let out a long, quivering whinny. The other horse answered in the same language.

"That's a queer way to talk to your friends," Pat said. "I'm glad I haven't got a voice like that."

"They only use that voice for shouting with," said Jerry. "When they want to talk quietly, they go close to each other and make little clicking sounds, so low you'd have to be near to hear them."

"I've heard them at it," said Pat. "It's maddening not to know what they're saying to each other."

"My father has strings of stories about people getting the gift of talking to the animals," Jerry said. He stopped talking and pointed. "Look there. That house up from the road would be a good place to start asking questions."

"We'll begin by asking for a drink of water," Pat said. "I could do with one."

A stream ran by the roadside in front of the house and widened into a little pool. They stopped for a few minutes there to let the horse drink. While they waited, a woman came to the open door of the house and watched them. As soon as the horse lifted his head from the pool, Pat turned him into the lane that led to the house and walked him as far as the door. By the time they reached it, a man had appeared beside the woman.

"God save all here," Pat said. "Can you spare us a drink of water?"

"We can, and a fine cup of tea," said the woman. "Come down off the horse and we won't be long making it."

"We haven't time, thanks all the same," said Pat. "We're on our way to Knock and it's still a long road. But we'd like the drink of water fine."

"And welcome, a-mac," said the woman, and she turned into the house to get it.

The man looked from one of them to the other curiously and said:

"What would be bringing you to Knock?"

"We're brothers," said Pat. "Our aunt is Mrs. Curran in Knock and we're on our way to see her. She's a widow woman and she can't leave the place. We're to stay a few days and maybe do a few things for her."

"And why are you riding Simon Folan's horse, if your aunt is Mrs. Curran in Knock? Simon has no relation of that name, in Knock or anywhere else."

"How do you know?"

"Sure, everyone knows that."

"Who said it's Simon Folan's horse?"

"Don't I know that horse as well as I know Simon himself, or my own son?"

"Have you heard any news of the ambush in Oranmore?" Pat asked quietly.

"Ah," said the man. "I have you now. We heard news of it, indeed. It was a great ambush and all the men are away safe. But there's a big search out for them, and the man that told us about it said that the Tans are out on the Cois Fhairrge road looking for a certain man that may have come this way. It's a good thing that you have Simon's horse, for you may need him if you find that man."

He cocked an eye at them and saw by their faces that they had understood him. Pat asked:

"Will everyone know the horse, all the way to Knock?"

"For a few miles more they might. He's a great horse. When we have the races again, we'll all put our money on him, especially if he has a national record by then."

At that moment his wife came out of the house with two mugs of buttermilk, one in each hand.

"I thought water was a cold sort of thing to give you," she said. "This will carry you better."

She watched anxiously for signs that they were enjoying it. When they had finished, she took the two mugs and said:

"Let you call in again on the way back."

"If you're not galloping too fast," said the man. "God's blessing go with you."

"May you go safe on the road," said his wife.

chapter 7

An Encounter with the Enemy

As they turned the horse out of the lane Jerry said:

"That man has a queer sense of humor."

"We got some news from him anyway," said Pat.

They trotted along for a while, thinking of the things he had said. Then Pat said:

"It's a fine thing to have the horse. From up here we can see the whole country."

"And the whole country can see us. Roddy will know the horse too, maybe. If he recognizes him, he may show himself."

But soon they found that they no longer felt pleased at being so high. Until now, all the stories they had heard of the Black and Tans had been like fairy tales of giants and wicked spirits and bogey men. Huddling around the fire on

winter nights, listening to those stories with shivers of terror, they had never really believed in them. They knew well
that when you turned a corner there was no real fear that
the three-headed giant or the eight-legged dog would be waiting there to swallow you whole. Even if these creatures had
once existed, you felt that it was in some bad old time before
the world was tidied up, and that it was extremely unlikely
that any of them would have survived until the present day.

With the Black and Tans it was different. One had to
believe in them. They were so called because they wore
black jackets and berets, and tan breeches. When they were
formed, there had not been enough garments of either color
to supply them with a proper uniform, so they had been
issued with a mixture of both. No sooner did they land in
Ireland from England than someone christened them with
the ironic name which had stuck to them ever since. It was
the name, too, of a well-known pack of hunting dogs near
Dublin, whose colors were also black and tan.

In Connemara and the islands, however, a strange thing
had happened. The name reached there by word of mouth,
of course, and the people thought that they were known in
Ireland as "The Blackened Hands," because their hands
were blackened with crime. This was translated into Irish,
and in many parts of Connemara where only Irish was
spoken, they were known as "Crúibíní Dubha." So every
time they were mentioned, one had a free reminder of their
reputation.

The boys had never seen them, because neither had been
to Galway since the war had begun. But the moment they
saw the cloud of dust away off on the road before them, they
knew who it was.

Pat reined in the horse.

"It's the Crúibíní," he said. "It couldn't be anything else.

The lorries raise the dust, I've heard the men say often."

"There's no hope of hiding. There's no place to hide."

"And there's no hope of running from them, with the weight of the two of us on the horse. The lorries would catch up to us."

"We don't want to run," said Jerry. "That would be no use. We want to get through to Knock."

"We have no choice now anyway," Pat said, "and that should make it easy."

He shook the reins and the horse moved nervously on. He had already seen the cloud of dust and was twitching his ears and dancing a little with fright.

"I think this fellow has never seen a lorry before," Pat said. "I hope he'll like it."

"I've never seen one myself," said Jerry, "and I know in advance that I'm not going to like it at all."

After that they were silent. The cloud of dust was moving nearer. They were passing through a place where there were no houses at all in sight. Bare rock, with tufts of grass and heather in the cracks, stretched away on their right-hand side. On their left there was a long, narrow, sedgy lake, with the mountains rising steeply behind it. Huge boulders were scattered on the mountainside. Jerry said:

"Only for the lake being in our way, we could have climbed a piece of the mountain and let them pass by. A horse could easily be hidden behind one of those rocks."

As Pat glanced across the gray water of the lake, he thought he saw someone move over there on the side of the mountain. The horse shied just then, at the sound of the roaring lorry engines, and it took all Pat's strength to hold him in. His front hoofs lifted off the ground and he let out an outraged whinny. Then the lorries came to a halt, blocking the road, and the engines were switched off. The horse pranced from side to side while the boys clung with their knees and their hands. All at once he stood still, breathing heavily, seeming to realize that there was no hope of breaking through the barricade.

There were three lorries. Slowly two of the Black and Tans climbed down on to the road from the leading one and walked forward. They were the biggest men that Pat had ever seen, as big as Martin Mór who was the recognized giant of all the islands. Their movements were deliberate and quiet, and as they came nearer they glared threateningly through narrowed eyes. Then the first one spoke:

"They're only boys."

The second one said:

"In Ireland they teach them treason young. Where are you going?" he snarled at them so suddenly and loudly that the horse's hoofs lifted again in fright.

"To Knock, to our aunt," said Pat in his best English. "This is my brother."

"Who is your aunt in Knock?"

"Mrs. Curran is her name."

The first one said:

"There's a Mrs. Curran in Knock, all right. Why are you going there?"

"To see her. She is a widow. She can't leave home to visit us."

"Where are you from?" The second man bared his teeth at them, like a dog, and a strange light seemed to start in his eyes. "Tell the truth or it will be the worse for you."

"From Mweenish, out beyond Carna," said Pat, starting back in terror, in spite of himself.

"Did you hear talk of an ambush in Oranmore?" the

first man asked, more quietly than the other. "Tell the truth, now. Don't be afraid. We won't hurt you, unless you tell lies."

"I don't even know where Oranmore is," said Pat boldly. This was indeed the truth. The second man said:

"Put them on the lorry and take them into Galway. I know that boy is not telling the truth."

Two of the crowd of men, who were leaning out of the lorries to listen, began to get down. The first man said:

"What do we want with two boys in Galway? We're not looking for boys. It doesn't look well to have boys as prisoners. They're too young to know anything. We'd better go on to Carna as we planned. There's a regular nest of rebels there, and there's a hotel where we can stop for the night."

The second man allowed himself to be persuaded, though he kept glancing suddenly at the boys as if he expected or hoped to catch them conspiring. Suddenly he slapped the horse's hindquarters letting out a tremendous roar as he did so:

"Go to Knock, then! Tell them——"

The rest was lost. The horse seemed to leap into the air. His front hoofs came up and pawed wildly. He gave a spring sideways and pranced several times on the same patch of grass at the roadside, while the boys clung with all their might to the saddle, to his neck, and to each other. Then he hurled himself forward past the stationary lorries in a huge bound which almost sent them sliding off backwards, and set off down the road at a furious gallop. The wind roared past their ears. Faintly they heard the men's shouts of laughter and the noise of the lorries' engines starting up. Still they clung to the horse, their mouths dry and their arms and hands sore. His gallop slowed a little, but there was a forward plunge to it that made them feel giddy. Then little

by little he slackened speed until at last Pat pulled him to a shivering stop.

They slid to the ground. There was no sound except the high singing of the wind and the far-off roar of the waves on the shore. They looked back along the road and saw that the lorries had moved on. Absentmindedly Pat pulled a handful of grass and rubbed the horse's neck with it. He was in a lather of sweat, with rolling eyes and fat pink tongue showing between his teeth.

"You're going to walk for a while, my boy," said Pat, "and so are we. I've had enough of riding."

"We got out of it well," said Jerry, "but my mouth is dry. We could all be in the ditch this minute. He's a great horse."

They pulled more grass and rubbed him down as well as they could, complimenting him in every way they could think of.

"If we walk him, he won't catch cold," Pat said. "Perhaps we'll come to a stream where he can drink. All the better if he has to wait a while."

Still there were no houses—only bog and rock and the brown mountain. The lake had finished in a mass of sedge and bulrushes. Walking was a strange sensation. Their legs felt weak and soft. The blowing dust of the road stung them. The dark was gathering heavily above them. It would be a dark night, they knew, with such dense black clouds shutting off the moon and the stars.

"If we have to travel in the dark," Pat said, "the horse will know where the road is. I think Knock can't be far ahead of us now."

The sight of the long road wearied them and presently they mounted the horse again. He seemed calm after his gallop and he waited patiently while they climbed onto him. The land became firmer, and after a while they found a clear stream by the side of the road. They let the horse drink there, and it seemed as if he would drink the stream dry. When he had finished, he ate a few mouthfuls of grass. Jerry watched him enviously.

"I wish I could do that——" Suddenly he stopped and began to rummage in the saddlebag. "The bread! The bread and the bacon that the decent woman gave us! I'd forgotten it."

"So had I," said Pat. "The heavens be her bed. A decent woman she is."

When they had eaten every crumb, they folded the cloth and put it back in the bag. Pat stretched his arms and then tightened his fists.

"Come on, now, all you Crúibíní!" he boasted. "I'm ready for ten of you!"

"A good job they can't hear you," said Jerry drily. "Even one of them would be too much for me."

Pat said:

"If they were anywhere around, you may be sure I wouldn't say the same thing."

The bacon had made them thirsty, but now they were afraid to lose time by getting down and drinking the water of the stream from their hands. Off in front of them they could see a few separated points of light as the lamps were lighted in the houses of a village. In spite of Pat's boasting of a moment ago, he began to feel weary and dispirited. The horse seemed to feel the same. Now he put down each foot slowly and carefully, like an old woman with corns wearing her Sunday boots. Very softly, Jerry began to sing the ballad that was in everyone's mouth these days:

When you honor in song and in story
The names of the patriot men
Whose valor has covered in glory
Full many a mountain and glen,
Forget not the gallant old west, boys,
Who rallied her bravest and best—
When Ireland was broken and bleeding,
She looked for good men to the west.

Pat felt himself heartened by this. He would have enjoyed singing the chorus with Jerry but he said instead:

"We'd better keep the rest of it until later. We shouldn't announce our arrival too loud. I'm sure this must be Knock."

They passed a cottage on the side of the road, so near that they could see right into the kitchen where a woman was stooping over the fire. At the sound of the horse's hoofs she turned her head quickly. They did not look back, though they knew she had come to the door to watch them along the road. A little farther on, a rutted lane led uphill on the left-hand side. At the top of it they could see a fine thatched house with two lighted windows and the door standing open.

"The wind must have changed," Jerry said. "The doors are open on the road side now."

"This could be Mrs. Curran's," said Pat. "The second house, well off the road. We'll try it."

He turned into the lane. It was almost dark now, and he had to let the reins go slack on the horse's neck so that he could pick his way wherever he chose. They passed between low walls and by a long turf-stack, then on to the flat, open space in front of the door.

At once, a woman came out onto the threshold. She stood

there, peering into the darkness. Then she said softly:

"Who is it?"

"Are you Mrs. Curran?"

"There are seven Mrs. Currans in Knock. Which one do you want?"

"The one that's our aunt. We're from Mweenish. We've come to visit our aunt because she's a widow and she can't leave home——"

"How many of you are there?"

"Two. Pat and Jerry."

"You'd better come inside," she said.

She came out and took the horse by the bridle while they dismounted stiffly. Without a word she led him into the shed at the end of the house and hitched his reins to a nail high on the wall. Then she went before them into the house and shut the door.

The white curtains were already drawn. There was a bright fire and a table partly laid for supper, but it seemed that the woman was alone in the house. The boys blinked in the lamplight while she looked them up and down. She was the same age as Pat's mother, very tall and thin, and with eyes so shrewd they seemed to see right into your mind. Suddenly she laughed and said:

"Every week I have new relations, all men or boys. Who sent you?"

"Our mother in Mweenish," said Pat, still careful.

"Did you by any chance come through Lettermore?"

"Yes," Pat said. "We came along the Cois Fhairrge road and a while back we met three lorry-loads of Crúibíní. They thought we might know something about an ambush in Oranmore."

"Are you Conneeleys?" she asked suddenly.

"I'm a Conneeley," said Pat, knowing at last that they could trust her. "We have a boat at Lettermore for my Uncle Roddy."

"Thanks be to God! And you got through the Black and Tans?"

Jerry said:

"Yes, but I wouldn't like to meet them again on the way back. We said we're staying a while in Knock."

"You saw no one on the road since?"

"Not a soul."

"The lorries went through Knock a few hours ago. They raided four houses but they took no one. They just took the women's wedding rings and gave out a few threats about burning the houses the next time, but that was all," Mrs. Curran said.

"They took their wedding rings!" Pat was shocked at this, knowing how his mother loved hers. Always in the evenings when she sat by the fire knitting, she kept turning her hand to watch it flash warmly in the firelight. She had told him once that when a woman has only one ring in the world, she loves it ten times as much as if she had a houseful.

"They always take the wedding rings," said Mrs. Curran, surprised. "Didn't you know that? Mine is gone long ago." She laughed rather sourly. "There's no use lamenting over things like that. I said to myself: 'May all the bad luck of the year go with it. It's the people that matter.'"

But they could see that she was hurt by it all the same. Pat said:

"Do you know where Roddy is? Have you seen him?"

"I've seen him but I don't know where he is now. Where did you meet the Tans?"

"By the lake, it was. Only for the lake we might have got away up the mountain."

"They'd have seen you and shot you down. Much better to face them, always. They're like dogs. If they see something running, they go to kill it, whatever it is."

"I hope we won't need your advice," said Pat. "Once is enough for me. When did you see Roddy? Was it since the ambush?"

"It was only an hour before the Tans came. I was out with the pigs after dinner, giving them their feed, and the next thing he came down the field behind the house, nice and brisk as if he were out walking the land on a Sunday afternoon. He came in and had some dinner and then he was off again. He wasn't more than half an hour in the house from start to finish."

chapter 8

Mrs. Curran

"So we're late," Pat said in a mournful tone, shaking his head.

He felt bitterly disappointed, though he could not have expected to find his uncle sitting at Mrs. Curran's table, waiting to be transported to Lettermore. He knew now that what he had really hoped for was that Roddy had not yet reached Knock, and that they could wait an hour or so for him and then lead him to the boat.

It was something at least to know that he was safe.

"Did he talk about the ambush?" Jerry asked.

"Yes, yes. It all went as they had planned it, and they didn't lose a single man."

"We heard that, from a man near Carraroe."

"The news traveled fast."

"Faster than we did. We should have been here when Roddy came."

"The world can't be planned that easy," said Mrs. Curran. "Tell me now, did you see no one at all as you came along?"

"You asked me that before," said Pat. "I only remember one sign of life after we left that house near Carraroe. While we were talking to the Black and Tans by the lake, there was someone over at the far side of it. Anyway, I saw somebody move."

Mrs. Curran asked eagerly:

"Was there good cover there?"

"There were rocks, big ones. I remember thinking that if we hadn't had the lake between us, we could have hidden the horse and all behind one of them."

"You saw *him* moving? Did the Tans see him too?"

"They were busy watching us. I don't think they noticed."

"Those fellows notice everything."

"They said nothing about it, though."

"That's a good sign, I suppose. What did they say to you?"

"One of the officers wanted to take us into Galway on the lorry, but the other said they'd go on to Carna instead."

"God help Carna! Did they say what they'd do there?"

"One of them said it was a regular nest of rebels."

Jerry imitated the Black and Tan's accent so perfectly that Pat chuckled.

"That's right," he said, "and he said they'd stay the night in the hotel."

"They'll play cards," said Mrs. Curran. "They love a game of cards. And they play for big money, I've heard. Even when they're not fighting, they want to keep up the excitement."

"They're in Carna now, I suppose," said Jerry.

"We can't be sure," said Mrs. Curran. "If we knew that they're there for certain, you could be on your way back to Lettermore this minute. You told them you're from Mweenish?"

"Yes, God forgive us. I was never in Mweenish in my life."

"It's out beyond Carna. Maybe they went out there. If they did, they'll meet their match, for once. The Mweenish people are as wild as hares and as hard to catch."

"They'll look for our mother there."

"Yes, but we never said what her name is," Jerry remembered.

"And you didn't mention Lettermore?"

"No."

"Then things could be worse," said Mrs. Curran. "Some Mweenish woman might even say she owns you, when she sees how the land lies. They're as clever as the bees out there. Now sit down to the table and start eating. A soldier never misses a chance of a meal."

While they were eating her soda-bread and butter, she asked them about the island, who was married, who was born or had died, and who had gone to America since she was there last. She had many friends on the island because her sister in Chicago had married an islandman there. They could never afford to come back to Ireland for a visit, so Mrs. Curran went to the island sometimes as their ambassador. She often went to Galway too, with her own horse and cart. It was fifteen miles each way, but the horse was young and strong, and unless it was raining she enjoyed going, she said.

"And I have friends in nearly every house on the way, where I could even stop for the night if I wanted to, but I always get back here safe enough. Now tell me, have you ever been to Galway?"

They had been there by sea only, of course, sailing into the Claddagh and tying up to the quay among the Aran and Claddagh and Connemara boats, sleeping in a Claddagh kitchen at night and walking around viewing the wonders of the town by day.

"But we haven't been there since the Black and Tans came," Pat said. "Do you think they'll be there forever?"

"They will not, faith," said Mrs. Curran. "This time the whole country is up. It's not like the old times when you'd have a rising in one county and the rest of the country wouldn't hear about it until it was all over."

"I wish they were gone out of the country," said Pat. "They're not like people at all—they're like some queer kind of animal. I hope I'll never lay an eye on them again as long as I live."

"I'm glad I saw them," Jerry said. "Now I'll know what the people are talking about. And I'm not half as frightened of them now as I was before I saw them. It's true that they're big, but I always imagined them twice that size. And I'm glad I saw the lorries. I wish we could have one of them on the island. It would carry ten donkey-loads of sea-weed without any bother at all."

Full of soda-bread and butter, the boys began to feel drowsy. Behind them on the hearth, the fire was all red and gave out a stifling heat. The wind was blowing in gusts around the house, but inside there was no sound except the steady, slow ticking of the big wall clock. It was blackened with age and smoke, and the long pendulum swung slowly back and forth so calmly that watching it would make a person fall asleep.

Then, in the silence, they heard a distant rumbling.

"Thunder," said Pat. "The storm will come back now."

Mrs. Curran got up quickly and went to the door. She opened it wide and the rumbling was instantly louder.

"That's not thunder," she said. "It's the Tans, coming back."

Now they could hear it plainly—a strange, regular sound as if the whole world had an engine inside it.

"Coming back? What will we do?"

Pat's first instinct was that they should put out the light and sit in the dark watching outward, like mice in their hole when the cat is prowling. But Mrs. Curran would not allow this.

"That sort of thing brings out the worst in them," she said. "Either they'll pass us by or else they'll come up here looking for you. If they come, you're my two nephews from Mweenish as you told them."

She left the door standing open and began to clear the supper things off the table. Then she calmly wiped off the flowery oilcloth that covered it, and rinsed out the cloth in a dish of water that stood on a table by the back door. Pat watched her as if he had never seen a woman do these things before. For the first time he saw that she must have been a real beauty in her day. Her hair was smooth and shining, chestnut brown with a few streaks of gray. Her forehead was high and smooth, and her eyes were as quiet as if nothing had ever happened in her life to trouble her.

While she was squeezing out the cloth she said:

"One of you could go to the door now and see what's happening. The lorries have stopped below on the road."

It was true that the rumbling was not dying away as it should have done if the convoy had moved on. Pat went to the door.

"They're at the house by the side of the road, where the woman came out to look at us," he said.

"If she tells them you came up here, perhaps they'll be satisfied and pass on."

Mrs. Curran picked up some knitting and sat in a chair half-facing the door.

"Now you can come over and sit on the hobs," she said. "Don't look frightened or they'll know you have something to hide. Keep your hands quiet and keep your eyes down. Don't let your foreheads wrinkle. God will protect us."

She was knitting a long black stocking and now she seemed suddenly to have become absorbed in turning the heel. The boys sat facing each other on the hobs at either side of the fire. They tried hard to follow her instructions, but when they heard shouts and the tramping of boots on the lane leading to the door, Pat could not prevent himself from leaping up and standing with his back to the wall by the fireside.

The first to come in were the two officers with whom they had talked earlier in the evening. They stared around the kitchen with narrowed eyes, twirling their revolvers between their fingers and thumbs. Mrs. Curran had stopped knitting. Jerry did not move. The fiercer of the two men marched over to Pat and said:

"So you got here, all right. What are you so frightened of?"

In the doorway more men were crowded, listening. Mrs. Curran stood up and said briskly:

"He'd be a queer boy not to be frightened of you yelling at him and waving your guns."

The other officer laughed and said:

"That's true, indeed. Put your gun away for the mo-

ment." He pushed his own into the holster. "You're Mrs. Curran?"

"Yes."

"These your two nephews?"

"Yes."

"Where are they from?"

"Mweenish."

"Outlandish name. What did you say? Mweenish? Where is it?"

"Out beyond Carna. Down by the sea. It's a few miles off the main road."

"Who is their mother?"

"My sister."

"Why did they come?"

"To do a hand's turn for me. My man died two years ago, in the big flu."

"They're staying here?"

"A few days only."

"How far are we from Galway?"

"Fifteen miles."

"Still fifteen miles! We should be in Carna now, sitting down to a fine supper, but we caught a rebel on the road back there and we had to turn around to bring him back into Galway."

Pat settled on the hob now and sat still, with his eyes down and his hands quiet, as Mrs. Curran had advised. As if she were in another room, he could hear her voice saying:

"You caught a man?"

"Yes. Skulking on the mountainside. We wouldn't have caught him if he hadn't fallen into a drain while we were chasing him. He didn't have time to get out before we were up with him. Said he was looking for his sheep. If it's true, he can go home tomorrow. We have instructions to bring in anyone that answers to a certain description—to compare with a photograph they have in Galway. I just wish we hadn't seen him before supper."

"Why don't you stop here and have supper?" Mrs. Curran said. "Sure, you must be starving with the hunger. The man is below on the lorry, well guarded I suppose."

"That's an idea. Have you food in the house?"

"I wouldn't have enough for the whole army of ye, but I'd have enough for five or six."

"That's not bad at all. The men can wait. They're used to it."

Now the two officers were smiling, like cats, Pat thought. Still numb from the shock of what they said, he watched in a kind of dream while they pulled chairs out from the table and sat down expectantly to wait for their supper. They beckoned to three others who were at the door and sent the rest down to the road to tell the men that there would be a delay.

Mrs. Curran made up the fire with good black turf and hung a kettle of water over it on the crane. Then she got out a piece of bacon and cut rashers from it, two for each man, and set them to fry in a big iron pan on the hearth. She gave Pat a fork to turn them with, while she took a bowl of eggs from the dresser. Soon she had a huge dish full of bacon and eggs, and as she set this on the table in front of the men she said in Irish:

"May it do you no good. A Christian can't say I hope it will poison you."

"What's that you said?" the officer asked suspiciously.

"It's a kind of prayer we say when we put the food on the table," she said calmly.

"Ah, yes, you Irish are full of prayers, though you're up to no good the rest of the time. And queer songs you have too."

"How do you know that?"

"I've heard the prisoners singing them on their way to jail—songs in Gaelic, like banshees wailing."

"Those are the old songs. I know a lot of them myself.

Let you be eating up now, and I'll sit by the fire there and be entertaining you with a bit of music."

"Fine, fine. But make it cheerful."

When she had cut bread for them and had made a big pot of tea, she settled in her chair again and picked up her knitting. She did not start work on it, however, but let it lie in her lap. Then she began to sing in a surprisingly sweet, strong voice, in Irish. The tune was one the boys knew well because it was very popular in all Connemara at that time. It had a slow rhythm and every line was decorated with grace notes and turns.

With the first words, they knew what she was doing. She sang:

Oh, boy, sitting there on my hob, you with the black hair,
Go out through the bedroom window in a little while and
*   unhitch your horse;*
There's a back way out of that shed and a lane that will take
*   you to the road.*
Go along the road to Furbo village, nine miles, and go to
*   John Walsh's house.*

She managed to make it sound like a real song by making the vowel sounds correspond at the end of each two lines. The boys were astonished at the contrast between her quick thinking and her calm appearance. When she drew breath for the second verse, one of the men said:

"That's not what I call cheerful."

Mrs. Curran took no notice. She went on singing:

Tell John Walsh that Ruairi is on the lorry with the Crúi-
*   biní,*
And if they get him in to Galway they'll know him from a
*   picture they have.*

*So the cars must be stopped at Furbo and Ruairi must be
        rescued tonight,*
*And when you have him safe, boy, you can bring him back
        here.*

"That's enough of that," said the first officer, happy with
his bacon and eggs. "Now we'll have something quicker."

"We will, so, if you don't like the old songs," Mrs. Curran
said, and she began on a lively love song about a young man
who ran away with a beautiful girl who was also rich. While
she was singing, Pat noticed that Jerry had laid his head
against the wall and was pretending to be asleep.

At the end of the second verse, Mrs. Curran said:

"Excuse me, before I go on with the music I'd like to
send the boys to bed. They're all day on the road and
they're worn out."

"We must be on our way too," said the second officer.
"It's eleven o'clock."

"What's your hurry. With those lorries you have, you'll
be in Galway in half an hour. Let you sit there a while, and
I'll get out the bottle and ye can have a drop to settle your
supper."

"We can wait, but only for a short while," the first man
said. "I could do with a drop."

Mrs. Curran shook Jerry's shoulder.

"Into bed, the two of you," she said. "You'll be up at
cockcrow in the morning for me. Off with ye, now."

She lit a candle for them and then she opened the big
drawer at the end of the kitchen table to get out a candle-
stick. To find it she had to lift out several things, and among
them was an old pack of playing cards. She left these casu-
ally on the table while she gave the boys the candle and
opened the bedroom door for them.

"Sleep sound," she said. "And don't be afraid. There's no one will go near you until the morning."

"That's right, boy," said the first officer, who had picked up the pack of cards and was beginning to shuffle them. "Sweet dreams."

The boys made no reply but went into the bedroom and shut the door.

chapter 9

An Ambush

Inside the bedroom, they stood perfectly still. The room was behind the fireplace. They had not been in it until now. They gazed around at it curiously.

It was bigger than the usual cottage bedroom, but it seemed to them that everything in Mrs. Curran's house was more substantial than in other Connemara houses. There was a double bed, a carved wooden chest, and a cupboard for clothes. There were curtains drawn close on the windows and the strangest thing of all was that there was a window to the back of the room as well as to the front.

" 'Tis a palace this house," Pat said in a whisper.

Through the door they could hear the voices of the men at their drink and their cards. Sometimes they heard Mrs. Curran's voice too but they could not make out the words.

The boys sat on the bed, close together as if they were cold. Jerry said:

"In five minutes' time I'll have to get out through that window and take the horse down to Furbo, as she said."

"Are you afraid?"

"No. I should be, but I'm not."

In the light of the candle Pat looked at him with amazement. It was true that he did not seem at all frightened. His eyes were shining and dancing, like someone who has been promised a very special treat.

"She told me to go," Jerry said. "I have the black hair. I'd rather be the one that goes than the one that stays."

There was no more time for talk then. They took the long bolster that was on the bed and arranged it as if it were a boy asleep—a boy who likes to sleep with his head quite under the bedclothes. Then they blew out the candle.

Instantly it was pitch dark, so dark that they felt they could scarcely breathe. Very carefully, Jerry slid across the catch of the back window and lowered the pane gently. The space that was now opened looked very small. The wind came sailing into the room. Pat said:

"Hurry. The men in the kitchen may notice the draft."

The night was so black that ten men could have been standing there waiting to catch Jerry as he crawled out and lowered himself to the ground. Later he told Pat that this was the worst moment of the whole night.

When he was sure that Jerry was safely outside, Pat climbed quickly onto the window sill and poked his head through the open space. He could hear Jerry moving softly to the gable of the house and fumbling at the bolt of the shed door. He waited for no more. The wind was whirling around the room behind him. Quickly he withdrew his head and lifted the window pane back into place.

He stood there in the darkness, listening so intently that he seemed for the time being to have been given extra hearing powers. Very faintly, through the thick wall that divided the shed from the bedroom, he could hear the horse's hoofs move slowly and cautiously on the stones. Then there was the sound of the shed door closing gently, more a feeling than a sound, and then no more. He listened and listened, until he realized that Jerry must be well along the lane at the back of the house.

Suddenly Pat felt a sensation of despair at being left behind. Jerry had said:

"I'd rather be the one that goes than the one that stays."

Now he knew that the hardest thing in the world was to get quietly into bed and lie down beside the bolster that should have been Jerry. But this was what he had to do. A shout of laughter from the next room reassured him that the men were enjoying their game. He lay on his back the better to hear them. The bottle was being pushed along the table and the voices were louder. Then he heard someone throw back his chair and tramp across to the bedroom door.

Pat lay as still as if he were dead. The handle rattled and the door opened an inch. A long shaft of light cut the room in two. Mrs. Curran's voice came strongly, much louder than was usual with her:

"Let you leave the poor boys to their sleep. There's neither one nor the other of them has music, my sister told me, so it's no good asking them to sing. Why don't you strike up a song yourself? You look like a man that would be a singer."

"He is, he is!" the other shouted. "Come on, George! Give us 'The South Down Militia.' Don't be shy."

"Oh, all right," said George, sounding pleased and bashful, like a girl.

And standing right there, with his back to the partly open door, he began:

I belong to a famous regiment whose deeds are often told,
For on the field of battle they were always brave and bold.

It had a strong marching rhythm and a chorus in which they all joined:

You may talk about your Scots Guards, Queen's Guards, and
  all,
You may talk about your Kilties and your Bonny Forty-
  Twa',
Or any other regiment under the Queen's command,
But the South Down Militia is the terror of the land.

At the end of the second verse, perhaps at a sign from Mrs. Curran, the door closed. Pat could still hear the singing but he could no longer make out the words. He stretched his stiff arms and legs and rolled over on his side so as to look like the bolster if one of the men were to think of peeping in. But he guessed that they would not do so now.

The time passed like a century. He had no way of knowing what time it was because the kitchen clock did not strike. Lying there in the warm darkness, he thought with agony of his uncle on the lorry, so near to him but so well guarded that he might as well be in the Galway jail. For a few wild seconds he began to plan how he would go to him and tell him that his rescue was planned, but then he realized that if he were caught the whole project might fail. And he would almost certainly be caught. Nine miles to Furbo, Mrs. Curran had said. A good horse would easily do this in an hour, if he were not delayed and if the rider knew the way. Then it would take time to organize the ambush. If the men of

Furbo succeeded in rescuing Roddy, it would take at least another hour for him and Jerry to come back to Knock. An hour, half an hour, an hour, an hour—he tried to add them up but for some reason he could not do it.

He dozed for a while and woke to hear the men stamping around the kitchen as they prepared to go. He lay quite still until the last shouts had died away.

"Good-by, good-by! Thanks for the food. Everything was fine except that wailing song of yours———"

Down on the road the engines growled, and then the whole convoy moved off. Pat sprang out of bed, as fast as if it had been a suddenly opened trap. He darted into the kitchen. Mrs. Curran was sitting at the table, white-faced with rage.

"They're gone," she said, "but they've left their ghosts behind. It will take a few days' airing to clear them out. Two and a half hours of them I had, after you went to bed."

"Enough for Jerry to get to Furbo."

"Plenty. I hope I won't have a party like that again for a while."

"They wanted us to sing for them?"

"They did. I nearly lost my life when that blackguard put his hand on the door."

"So did I," said Pat drily. "Jerry was gone by that time. How did you guess that man could sing?"

"He had the legs of a lark," said Mrs. Curran sourly. Then she began to laugh. "He sang that song right well." And she began to sing softly:

When Kruger heard the regiment was landed in Cape Town,
De wet, says he, we're bet, says he, they've sent for the South Down.

The cards were thrown in a long line on the table. The air was heavy with tobacco smoke. An empty bottle stood in the middle of the table and stained glasses were ranged around. Pat knew what Mrs. Curran meant when she said the ghosts of the men were still there. He helped her to clear the things off the table and wipe it clean.

"It was well you thought of singing the message to us," he said, "and lucky they let you sing."

"Lucky, indeed, but if they hadn't I'd have started on some prayers in Irish, or I'd have managed to find some other way."

"None of them has Irish?"

"No, and there's many a time it would have been useful to them. The worst of it for me was that that's the first time I sang since my husband died, God rest him. I used to be always singing, at every wedding and party, but I thought I'd never do it again."

"When you did, it was in a good cause."

They opened the front door to let the clean air blow in. Pat went out on the step to get the feel of the wind on his face. There was a brightness in the sky now, as if the dawn were not far away. Only one light showed, in the house down by the road. Mrs. Curran said:

"Let you make up the fire and I'll run down and ask my neighbor how she got on with the men that were told to wait below. All night I'm thinking of her, but there was nothing I could do that wouldn't make it worse for both of us."

While she was gone, Pat built up a fine fire from the little turf-stack that stood against the wall. Then he hung a kettle of water on the crane, brushed up the hearth, and sat on the hob to wait for her to come back.

The water was hissing into the ashes from the kettle's

spout before he heard her step in the lane. As she came in at the door she said:

"Things could have been worse. They made her bake bread for them, and they ate every bit and scrap of food she had in the house, but they didn't harm her, nor the children. I told her to bring them all up here for breakfast in the morning. She said it wasn't blessings the men were throwing after their officers, and they knowing well the fine time they were having up here, but they didn't dare to do anything about it."

"Did she hear any word about Roddy?"

"She knew that they had someone on the lorry that they were very precious about. She said they didn't give him a bite to eat, the poor man—only ate it all themselves. They asked about her husband and she told the truth, that he died in the big flu two years ago like my own man, God rest them both. She didn't say that if he was alive he'd be out on the hills fighting, with the best of them."

She made tea, and they sat on by the fire until the curtains turned white on the windows as the dawn came up. They were silent for a long time, leaning back in their corners drowsily.

It was Mrs. Curran's horse that roused them. From away up in the field behind the house, they heard him give a strong whinny, like a wild laugh. They sat up, the better to listen. Mrs. Curran said:

"It could be that he has seen the Lettermore horse. He's nearly like a dog, that horse of mine, for letting you know if there's someone coming."

They went out by the back door and paused for a moment. The sky was higher than it had been yesterday, and the clouds were not so black, but the whistle had come back

into the wind. The sea in the distance was lead colored,
misty with spray. It was no more than four o'clock, and bit-
ter cold.

They saw the horse and its two riders move slowly down
the green lane that led to the back of the house. Silently
they waited while it came nearer and nearer. Roddy sat
in the saddle and Jerry sat forward on the horse's shoulders,
his back straight and his head up as if he had had a long
night's rest in bed.

"Here ye are, my two fine heroes," Mrs. Curran said

softly when they were near enough. She took the horse's reins and held him while they dismounted. "Into the stable with him, Pat. He has a long road before him yet."

Pat trotted the horse into the stable and hitched him quickly to a hook. Then he ran back to the kitchen so as not to miss any of the account of what had happened.

As he came panting in at the door, Roddy was saying:

"We have ten minutes and no more. A drink of water is what I'm longing for."

While he and Jerry were drinking, Mrs. Curran said:

"You're safe. You weren't wounded."

Roddy laughed. "It was a queer ambush," he said. "The Furbo men couldn't have spared any ammunition to wound us with. When the lorries stopped below on the road early in the evening, first of all I thought the Black and Tans had got on to you somehow or other. I thought that any minute I'd see you being marched down the lane between them and that we'd be traveling in to jail together. Then one of the Tans let it out, in talk between themselves, that the officers were gone up to find out if the boys had told the truth about where they were going."

"Go back a bit further," Mrs. Curran said. "How did they catch you in the first place? When you left here yesterday, I didn't think you'd be back to me so soon."

"Neither did I," Roddy said. "I was way up above the road, well out of sight, until I came to Loch Riach. Then I had to move down a bit toward the lake, because the mountain is treacherous with bog. On my way down I saw the convoy and I saw them stop the two boys on the horse. I thought they were faring badly, so I let myself be seen, to draw the Tans away. As it happened, the boys did better than I did. Immediately after they had got away, the Tans spotted me and they gave chase. I ducked all their shots, and they'd never have caught me if I hadn't fallen into a drain."

"They told us that."

"So back we came along the road and I had no way of warning anyone that might have stopped the lorries and rescued me. If they'd got me in as far as Galway, I'd have been in a tight corner, with that photograph they have."

"Tell about the ambush."

"Ambush, you call it!" said Roddy. "But it served well enough."

Jerry said:

"John Walsh laughed when I told him that he and the men of Furbo were to ambush the convoy of lorries as it came on the Spiddal road. 'We couldn't ambush a flock of geese,' he said to me, 'not to mind a few lorry-loads of Crúibíní all armed to the teeth.' 'So you're going to let them pass through, then,' I said, 'with Roddy, and they'll make mincemeat of him when they get him in to Galway.' 'Wait, wait,' he said, 'and give me a chance to think. I'll have to talk to the lads.' "

"How did you find his house?" Pat asked.

"No trouble at all. You'd nearly think the Furbo people were expecting me, or else they never go to bed at all there. The first house I went to, a man came with me and showed me the way to John Walsh's door. He was up and about, though it was after midnight, and he went the rounds then and there and collected a fierce-looking crowd of his friends with all kinds of queer old guns. They said some of those guns were at the Crimean War, but maybe they were pulling my leg."

"They were not," Roddy said. "It was handy, in a way, to have the old guns because every one of them made a noise like a cannon going off."

"They all went along the Spiddal road, about two miles," said Jerry, "and they put myself and the horse up a lane at the side away from the sea. They told me the lane went up the hill for a mile and a half and that there was an old road through the bog after that, if I could find it. That was all they could do for me, they said.

"I thought the lorries would never come. I was sitting there on the horse for an hour or more. I knew they had rolled a few big rocks from the walls out into the middle of the road. That would be enough to stop the lorries, they said. They all went in behind the walls then, to wait. There weren't any houses near. The night was so dark and the wind was so strong, I couldn't see where the men were nor hear them talking.

"One of them must have been up the hill on the lookout, for I heard a whistle when the lights of the first lorry came into view. From where I was I could see them moving along, and I held the horse in hard in case the noise would frighten him.

"It was well I did. He pranced around as if he were mad when the lorries stopped on the road in front of the rocks. But no one heard his hoofs pounding because the engines had been left running. The Crúibíní all jumped out, yelling and roaring, and the Furbo men fired their guns and did a bit of yelling too, I think."

"They did, faith," said Roddy. "They yelled to me in Irish to get off the lorry and run for my life. That's what I was doing, anyway. I had no sooner got my feet on the ground than one of the Furbo men had a hold of me and was dragging me away to where the horse was. I got up in front of Jerry and we were away."

"Is that all you saw of the ambush?"

"Wasn't it enough? We stopped again high up on the

hill to change places, for the horse's comfort as well as our own. We looked down to see what was happening. By that time the lorries were just beginning to move on. I think what happened was that the Furbo men all just disappeared when they knew I was away. They hadn't the weapons nor the ammunition for a real ambush. It would have been no use to try to carry on with it."

"They must have the courage of lions," Mrs. Curran said, "to have gone at all."

Roddy said:

"They're good men, and they planned it well. No one will know exactly where they came from because the place they picked is a long way from anywhere. They probably went home across country and were back in their houses if the Tans raided them on their way in to Galway. But the Tans may be out after you, Mrs. Curran. You'd better take a holiday with your sister in Mweenish for a few days. Jerry told me all about her. Your neighbor below can say you brought the boys back."

"If I hear any more about that sister, I'll nearly begin to believe in her," said Mrs. Curran. "I'll go over to Moycullen to my cousin for a while, till I hear they have no more interest in me or in my relations. After all the poteen they drank and all the bacon and eggs they ate, they should be my friends for life."

chapter 10

Home to
the Island

For the journey back to Letter-
more, they had to take Mrs. Curran's horse. He was in good
spirits because he had not had an outing for ten days, when
Mrs. Curran had brought a load of new potatoes to Galway
on the cart. She had an ancient saddle, hanging on a peg in
the stable. It had not been used for years, but the girths were
in good order and that was all that mattered.

"Two should ride the fresh horse," Mrs. Curran said.
"The Lettermore horse will have enough to do to carry one
person. He's done a fine night's work."

When they led him out of the stable, he kept his head
down as if to watch his tired feet lift slowly one by one. But
when he found himself faced for home, he seemed to
brighten up.

Pat said:

"You'll have a week's holiday after this, my boy. You can be boasting to every horse in Connemara of what you've been doing."

At that hour of the morning, no one was stirring. Still they kept the horses on the grassy verge of the road to lessen the sound of their hoofs. Jerry rode the Lettermore horse, and Pat and his uncle had Mrs. Curran's. As first they could see the sea to their left, but presently a rocky stretch of flat, gray land came between. There were some scattered houses down there, but the chimneys had not yet begun to smoke. Ahead of them the road stretched unendingly. Pat wished he were back on the island where he knew every hill and hollow, every rock and stone, every road and lane. One would never come to know a district as big as the one they were passing through now, he thought. And there were so many people and houses, you could not possibly trust everyone you met.

"Will you stay long with us?" he asked Roddy. "You'll be safe on the island."

"I know that," said Roddy, "but there are more important things than to be safe. I'll be a week or two, I'm sure. When Michael Cooney comes with the plans for the big ambush in Clifden, we'll go over them together and we'll be off."

"Michael Cooney? Our teacher?"

"Yes, of course."

"He's coming back?"

"For a visit only. He'll come away with me again. I know now that this time we're going to succeed. If we can hold out for a short while more, we'll have peace in the country at last."

Passing by the lake, Roddy showed them the point on the hillside above from which he had watched them talking to

the Black and Tans. The sandy road still bore signs of having been trampled by many feet. The Lettermore horse
shied tiredly as he remembered the place.

After that Pat found that it was a torment to be so high,
on view for miles. He would have liked them to leave that
road and take a byroad down to the sea, and so make their
way around to Lettermore. But Roddy said:

"We must take the quickest way. If we go in a round-
about way, we might arrive in Lettermore and find the Tans
there waiting for us."

"You think they'll come out again?"

"I don't know. It could happen. Perhaps Mrs. Curran's
poteen will have given them headaches, so that they won't
feel like coming out early."

At the house where they had received their first news of
the ambush, there standing on the roadside was the man
who had recognized Simon Folan's horse.

"Ye're back safe," he called out as soon as they were near
enough, "and the horse is in good order." He looked with
interest at Roddy. "You'd be Roddy Conneeley from the
island." When Roddy made no reply, he went on: "Don't
take too much notice of me. I was always a curious kind of a
man. When you'd live out in a quiet place like this, especially if you're curious, you'd like to know the name of
everyone that would pass by."

"You can forget my name again now, as fast as you
guessed it."

"Easy, easy," said the man. "No need to fly at me. If the
Tans come by here, I'll send them on the long, hard road to
Letterfrack. And I'll tell you something else: everyone
along the road will speed them on their way."

The last part was shouted after them as they moved away
from him. Roddy said:

"His kind are all talk. They won't lift a finger for us, for fear of losing their few sticks of furniture or their half dozen hens. I'll tell you something important, Pat. If people are very poor, it knocks all the spirit out of them. In the end, they don't know whether they're being kept in slavery or not, they're so used to it. That man knows we're fighting for him and for everyone like him, but still he stays well out from us. And he'd even criticize our methods, if he felt like it. You know the old saying: the best hurler is the one on the ditch."

At last, from the top of a rise, they were able to look down at Lettermore. By now the house doors were beginning to open and smoke to come from the chimneys, blown in every direction by the wind. As they clattered across the bridge that led onto the island of Lettermore, spray from the seething waves drenched them to the skin. The cold of it shocked them awake. The roar of the waves filled the air like thunder.

Roddy said:

"It's an ugly morning for a sail."

"With three Conneeleys on board we'll be safe enough," said Pat, and he told him the story of the seals that had guided them into the harbor.

As they approached Matthew Folan's house, Mike came out and started down toward the harbor. Suddenly he lifted his head and saw them, and then he turned and ran back, seeming to fly over the ground instead of touching it with his feet. By the time they reached the house, there was a whole group waiting to help them down off the horses, and look them over to see if they had suffered any damage, and urge them to come into the kitchen and eat breakfast while they told what had happened.

Morgan could not keep still as he listened. He walked up

and down the kitchen between the fireplace and the door until at last Roddy said:

"Sit down here, Father, and rest yourself a while. We have a long road before us yet."

"The boat is all ready," Morgan said. "We can go any moment we like."

But he sat down at the table all the same and gazed at Roddy as if he had never seen him before. When all three had finished telling their stories, old Matthew Folan said to Jerry:

"You did a hero's part. What is your father's name? Maybe I know him."

"Owen Lynskey," said Jerry very quietly.

"Lynskey? Lynskey?"

"That's right. My great-grandfather was the informer."

There was a short silence. Then Roddy said sharply:

"Are they still saying that?"

"Yes. And they'll never stop until our seed and breed dies out."

"They'll stop," said Roddy. A moment later he stood up and said:

"We'd best be on our way. We'll have to leave you Mrs. Curran's horse. It's no use sending him back yet, until you hear she has come home from Moycullen."

"God speed you," Mrs. Folan said. "You'll be back to us before long."

She did not come down to the quay because, she said, the sight of them embarking on that terrible sea would be enough to make her faint. But everyone else went, even old Matthew Folan, who could not get over his astonishment that Morgan at his age should be prepared to set out on it.

"But you were always a great sailor, Morgan, though you were in another trade altogether."

"Maybe that's why I had to get good at it," said Morgan, "to be as good as the real sailors."

He promised to come back and visit his friend again in calmer weather. He gave a little chuckle and said:

"Ten years ago I thought I was too old to sail any more. It wasn't that I was afraid, but I thought I wouldn't be strong enough. It's a mistake not to do a thing just because you're afraid you won't succeed. I've learned that much from this week's work."

And he stepped aboard the hooker as if the sea and the sky were blue instead of black, as if there were a gentle breeze instead of the wicked storm that tossed the boat up and down, even at the quay.

The moment they cast off, with the reefed mainsail only, the hooker plunged away from the wall. They could hear the voices of Simon Folan and his father calling after them but their words were caught and carried away by the wind at once. It seemed suddenly to have become much colder, and Pat could feel the wind cutting through his wet clothes so that he shivered as if it were the middle of winter.

Then he remembered that James Fitzmaurice had said there were dry jerseys on board. Now that Roddy was there to help sail the boat, he was able to take time to open the locker forward and take out the bundle that was there. He found three jerseys of various sizes, so that he and Roddy and Jerry could have one each. Mike's and Morgan's had been dried in the Folans' kitchen.

After that Pat went to stand with Mike, ready to carry out any order given by Morgan, who was at the tiller. They were tacking across the bay, making for the open sea. It was half-tide, and now the low towers that marked the channel were plainly visible. At his elbow Mike said:

"I wonder when I'll get a chance of a sail again."

He sounded so sad that Pat looked at him in astonishment. The hooker was moving out from the little shelter afforded by the land and she was beating her way through the boiling sea in a series of long, painful tacks, so that it was clear the journey back to the island was going to be slow.

"Perhaps you'll have enough of sailing by the time we get to the island," he said.

"Not if I lived twice over," said Mike.

And all the way through the whole of that long and cruel journey, the look of ecstasy never left his face.

By the time they reached the island, Pat had almost determined never to set foot in a boat again. They were less than a mile from it before it came into view. It seemed to be circled with a white ring, where the waves broke on its stony beaches and against its cliffs and reefs. Spray shot high into the air in tall spouts that scattered and blew over the land like rain. At first they could not see anything through this mist, not even the houses that were nearest to the slip. Then as they came closer, gradually they became aware that a crowd was gathering there, growing every moment bigger and bigger.

"It looks like everyone on the island is down to meet us," Morgan called out.

The boom swung across as he brought the boat around.

"I'm taking the same course back that I took on the way out," he said to Pat, and he gave a little chuckle, like a satisfied hen. "Long ago when I used to be sailing over to Connemara, the other men used to ask me how I knew what the wind was doing, and one day I told them it's how I see it. I'll never forget the way they laughed at me—years after, they were still laughing about the man that could see the wind. But it was true, in a way, that I could see it—or if I couldn't, I knew so much about it that there was no need to see it. With sail up and your hand on the tiller, you can feel every move it makes and there's not much difference between feeling and seeing."

After that there was no more time for talk. In any case it would not have been possible to hear. The wind seemed to have grown louder, or else it was that its continual beating around them, since they left Lettermore, had started a roaring in their ears. And the sea gulls seemed all to have gone suddenly crazy. A cloud of them circled the hooker, giving off piercing screams. They dived in the air and went floating up again, like fish in the sea. Right into the slip they followed them, so that it was as if they arrived home with a strange and weird-sounding band.

The waves ran all the way up the slip and poured off it again in a shining waterfall. Ankle-deep in water, James Fitzmaurice was waiting to moor the boat. Pat saw his mother, high on the beach, well away from the sea, and Mike's mother clinging to her as if she were in terror of her son's drowning even now. He looked about for his father but at first he could not find him. Then, after a moment, he saw him at the back of the crowd that stood on the beach out of reach of the waves. He had Owen Lynskey by the arm and was urging him forward, leading him toward the slip.

They reached it just as the boys stepped ashore. Roddy was already moving up the slip, deep in talk with James Fitzmaurice. At the top they met Jim and Owen. Owen seemed to be hanging back, almost dragging his arm away from Jim's grasp. Pat heard his father say:

"Roddy, this is Owen Lynskey, down to see his son land safe at home."

Roddy seized Owen's reluctant hand and shook it heartily.

"Lynskey? But for your son, this moment I'd be inside in the jail of Galway, waiting for my last hour." A gasp of astonishment went up from all the people who had pressed forward to listen. "We have long evenings before us for telling our story, and you'll hear all about what he did."

And holding Jerry on one side of him and Owen on the other, he marched up the road to his father's house.

Just as their mothers came flying down the beach to them with cries like sea gulls, Pat said to Mike:

"Jerry will get the hero's portion at home today, all right. I wonder how we'll fare ourselves."

But old Morgan was there in time to defend them. Before either of the women could start telling them what a wicked thing they had done in going off without leave in a raging storm, the old man said calmly:

"It takes a fine woman to rear a fine son. The two of ye can be proud of these two boys. If ye hadn't taught them courage and endurance in the cradle, they wouldn't ever have been able to serve their country as they did. It's the mothers of Ireland that should get the credit for all the heroes we've reared in the last seven hundred years."

Pat thought that this time it was the seals that should get the credit. They had led them into the quay at Lettermore, and Pat himself would never have thought of setting out in the storm if he had not expected their protection. However, this was no time for him to interrupt, while his grandfather was gazing as blandly as a baby at the two angry mothers.

They looked doubtfully at each other. They could not work this out quickly enough, and it was clear that they thought it unsafe to say anything until they had had time to think. Morgan went on:

"Now we'll go home, and you can get us the newest of food and the oldest of drink, the way they used to do for the old heroes of long ago, in Owen's stories. Food comes before drink and drink comes before talk, the old proverb says."

The two women hurried off to begin cooking. Morgan looked at the two boys and gave one quick wink. Then the crowd closed in around them and they all started up the hill together.